In memory of my beloved Rags

A Friendship for Today

PATRICIA C. McKISSACK

SCHOLASTIC INC.
NEW YORK TORONTO LONDON AUCKLAND SYDNEY
MEXICO CITY NEW DELHI HONG KONG BUENOS AIRES

ISBN-13: 978-0-545-06563-4
ISBN-10: 0-545-06563-1

12 11 10 9   10 11 12 13/0

Printed in the U.S.A.   40

First Scholastic paperback printing, January 2008

CHAPTER ONE

Last Day Forever

Friday, June 4, 1954

1954

Dwight D. Eisenhower is the president of the United States.

A first-class postage stamp costs 3 cents.

A new Studebaker car costs $1,700.

A gallon of gas is twenty-two cents.

A box of grits costs 8 cents.

A loaf of bread is seventeen cents at Mr. Bob's Grocery Store.

And today is the last day forever at Attucks Elementary. The Kirkland Board of Education announced the other day that the colored school will be closed and the students will be sent to John Adams Elementary and T. Thomas Robertson Elementary, all because the Supreme Court says there can't be any more segregation.

I'm remembering that morning in May — a month ago — when I came down to breakfast. It was like any other day. I put butter and sugar on my grits. The newspaper rustled when Mama turned the page. She took a sip of coffee and her face lit up like a Christmas tree. "At last! No more separate and totally unequal! No more overcrowded classrooms, outdated books, or not enough books. Oh, praise God from whom all blessings flow!" Daddy was just as happy. My folks had been attending meetings for over two years, trying to get Kirkland schools to integrate. Now they'd won.

But I was all the time thinking. "If white people want to go to school with us so much, seems to me all they needed to do was ask. We'd make room for a few white kids at Attucks Elementary next year. Why did it take the Supreme Court to figure that out?"

Mama stopped reading. At first she was quiet. Then she burst out laughing. In fact, she laughed so hard, her shoulders were shaking. "Rosemary, you are something else, girl!" she exclaimed.

"Why do you say that, Mama?"

"Oh, just the way you think. It's different."

"Do I think silly or something?"

"No, no. Being different isn't wrong. You're just fine. I know all of these changes must be terribly confusing. But next year when you are in a better school, you'll come to appreciate why this decision is so important."

"I hope so," I said, still feeling uncertain.

"Just keep marching to your own drum," Mama replied. "I love that about you, child."

Mama says things I don't always understand, like marching to my own drum. What drum?

As long as I can remember, everybody dresses up for the first and last days of school. I've always worn my Easter outfit on Report Card Day. But my Easter dress is pink organdy — Mama's idea of what a girl should wear. Mama makes beautiful clothes for me and for women all over Kirkland. And it's not that I don't like being dressed up. I do. But bows and sashes aren't my style.

So since I get to choose, I pick out my blue-and-white checked suit with the navy blue short-sleeved jacket to match. Maybe Mama'll let me wear my hair down. That's the one thing girly I like. "Please, Mama," I beg.

"When you're older," she says, pulling the comb through my thick, curly hair.

"I am older. See how tall I am?" I stand on my toes.

But Mama's mind is made up. She pulls my hair back into a single ponytail and ties it with a piece of light blue ribbon. She chuckles. "Being tall doesn't make you older," she says. "When you are in junior high school, we'll talk about wearing your hair down."

"But that's forever away," I argue.

Turning me around, Mama looks me in the eye. "Rosemary, don't be overly dramatic. Do you really know how long forever is?"

"A long, long, long, long time."

Mama comes back with, "Your time as a child is short." I can mouth the words as she says them. "So stay a child as long as you can, because you're going to be an adult . . ." Then together we say, "Forever." Mama tickles me on both sides, adding, "Hey, look, you're almost too big for this suit."

"I'm the tallest one in my class," I say proudly.

"The tallest girl?"

"No, ma'am. The tallest of all — boys and girls," I answer, adding, "Only person who is taller than me is Mrs. Washington. And I can outrun everybody, too."

Mama smiles. "Even Mrs. Washington?"

"I've never raced my teacher, so I don't know, but I'm thinking I might win . . . and without a head start." The idea makes me smile.

Mama laughs. It's good to see her in such a good mood. She doesn't smile much, and rarely laughs these days. And even when she does, her eyes still look sad.

"Girl, I don't know where you're getting all this height," Mama says, turning me 'round and 'round. "The Pierce folks on my side are short and the women on your daddy's side aren't too tall, either."

I stand back-to-back with Mama. Even though I'm only ten — going on eleven — and getting ready to go into sixth grade — if I pass — I'm up to Mama's shoulders already. "If I'm this tall now, when I get to be sixteen I'll probably be taller than you, Mama!"

"I don't care how tall you get, you'll still be my baby girl," she says, giving me a hug. "Come on, eat your breakfast." She shakes her head in disbelief.

"Is Daddy up yet?" I ask.

Mama stumbles over her words. "No! Yes, yes. Well, no, he's not here."

That's Mama's way of getting around saying that Daddy didn't come home last night — again. I don't know why she tries to hide it from me. Our house is too small. I can see and hear everything that's going on. A deaf, dumb, and blind man would know things are not right between them.

I take a gulp of milk as I slide into the chair by the window. I can watch the birds and wave at my friend and neighbor, J.J. Stenson. There's a big oak between our houses and J.J. and I put birdhouses in the tree this spring so we both can bird-watch from our kitchen windows. He calls the tree a "bird hotel," because so many birds live there.

James Johnson Stenson, Jr., is a rare bird himself. Nobody ever calls him James or Jim. He's been J.J. ever since we started kindergarten together.

I sometimes think J.J. stands for "Jumping Jack" Stenson, because he's never still. He gets into trouble all the time for not being at his school desk when the bell rings. Half the time he hasn't done his homework. He does just enough to squeak by. Still, he's fun to be around and everybody likes him. So much so, he was elected class vice president. I'm the president this year. I figure that means my classmates like me, too. I guess.

Aunt Betty is at the sink in front of her window. She waves at me. No sign of J.J. this morning.

Betty and J. Johnson Stenson, Sr., are not my real aunt or uncle, but they are my parents' best friends-like family. Mama's old-timey and strict about courtesy, minding, and back-talking. I'm not allowed to call grown-ups by their first names — without a "handle," as Mama calls it. So J.J.'s parents are Aunt Betty and Uncle John. J.J. calls my folks Aunt Doris and Uncle Mel. I can get away with a lot, but the moment I try to sass, I'm on punishment, quick-like. No radio shows for a week.

Mama begins to clear the table. That's my cue that it's time to leave for school. "Hurry up, now, or you'll be late for Report Card Day."

I slurp down the rest of my milk, wipe my mouth, and put the dishes in the sink. "I'm going by the shop after school to show Daddy my grades," I say.

Mama's eyes change from honey-brown to dark brown. They always change color in dim light or when she's upset about something. "Don't be disappointed if he's not there," she says. "Maybe your father can see your grades when he comes home."

"*If* he comes home," I say under my breath.

Mama's eyes darken even more. She almost speaks, but thinks better of it. Throwing me a kiss instead, she waves good-bye. "See you later," she says. Her eyes appear to be pools of dark water ready to spill over.

Beverly Enge and J.J. are waiting for me at the corner of Harrison and Rosebud streets, same as usual. Reliable Bevvy. Back when we were in kindergarten, Mama and Aunt Betty hired Bevvy, who was then in sixth grade, to see that we crossed Kirkland Highway safely. We'll be in sixth grade next year. Still, Bevvy is on the payroll and continues to take her job seriously.

"I didn't see you at the table this morning," I say to J.J.

"I ate earlier, because I woke up at first light. Couldn't sleep, 'cause I'm too worried," he explains. "I've got to get promoted. I can't get held back."

"You should have been thinking about that all year," says Bevvy, sounding like a mama. She taps him on the back of his head. "You play too much."

"Beverly! Stop that." I know him. He's annoyed and embarrassed.

"You'll pass," I say. But I'm not nearly as sure as my words. "You'll get by. You always do."

J.J. is really my best friend, even though neither one of us will admit it. I can't remember a time when there wasn't a J.J. in my life. He's got two younger brothers — Bootsie, who is four, and Josh, who is two. I don't have any siblings, so the Stenson brothers are like real kin.

We pass by Mr. Bob's Grocery Store and Bevvy goes in to buy a pack of Juicy Fruit chewing gum. She loves Juicy Fruit because it pops better than other brands. Bevvy should know, because she's a pro at popping gum. In fact, she cracks it so loud sometimes it sounds like a gunshot. Smacking gum gets on Mama's nerves so bad, she would fall down in a fit if I did it.

Mr. Bob sees us from his front window and waves. He's a big man with a booming voice to match his size. As long as I can remember he has taught Sunday school at the Mount Olive African Methodist Episcopal Church. He tells us wonderful stories about David and the giant, wise King Solomon, Daniel and the lions, but he also tells us about Frederick Douglass, Harriet Tubman, Sojourner Truth, and other great Negroes in our history. He's very smart. Nobody could have worked harder for integration than Mr. Bob Mason.

His wife, Miz Lilly Belle Mason, is equally nice. Her beauty shop is on the other side of the grocery store. Mama goes to Miz Lilly Belle for a wash, press, and curl every two weeks. I can't wait until I can go to the beauty shop regularly.

"Race you to the stop sign!" J.J. says.

"No!"

"Why?"

"Because you make me sick," I say, wishing a hundred times I'd never made that silly promise — the one J.J. has held me to all year. When school started last September, I made J.J. a promise that I'm still bound to keep. Perhaps it's because my legs are longer, but I'm faster than he is, no matter what the distance — long or short. What makes it so bad is I am the only person who can really outrun him. So one day when we were sitting on the porch together, he asked me all pitiful-like, "Would you do me a favor? Don't beat me in front of the boys. They'll never let me forget it. You can beat me all you want when it's just you and me racing, but please don't beat me in front of everybody."

Baloney! (That's my special word, because it says a whole lot more than I dare speak.)

It's so like J.J. to worry about what the boys will think. Who cares? But since it seemed important to him, I agreed. "Okay. But I won't cheat and deliberately lose. I just won't race you."

"Promise?"

"Promise! Cross my heart and hope to die."

J.J. knows that I don't go back on promises. But J.J. loves to tease and it's usually me he's teasing. First thing, he starts mouthing off in front of the boys. "What's the matter, Rosemary, you scared of me? You know I can run circles around you. . . ."

Silly boy!

Since he can outrun every kid in fifth grade, they honestly believe his big talk. Oooooweee! I can't wait 'til I'm out of this promise and I can finally show him up.

My biggest regret about the whole promise thing though is the ruckus it caused between Mama and Daddy. They got started and the arguing hasn't stopped yet.

I remember the big blowup as though it were yesterday. I'm still analyzing what happened, over and over, searching for what might have caused such a simple conversation to turn so sour.

Here's what happened. We were having dinner when I told Mama and Daddy about the promise I made to J.J., and that he was bragging about being the fastest kid in class when it's really me who's the fastest. Suddenly, Mama hit the table with her fists. The silverware bounced and the glasses wobbled. "You promised what?" she shouted.

"It's nothing," I said, all the time wondering why Mama was so upset.

"But it *is* something," Mama added. "It's a dangerous pattern you can let yourself fall into . . . holding back . . . putting others before yourself. You should leave him in the dust," Mama said. Her voice was loud and angry as she slathered butter on her roll. "Don't hold back on account of you're a girl. Never be afraid of being better than a boy. If you can honestly beat him, then don't be dishonest with yourself and lose."

By then, I was wishing I'd never opened my mouth. Daddy always worked hard, but lately he'd been working extra hours, not getting home until way after my bedtime or maybe not at all. He's a mechanic who owns his own shop — Mel's Able Auto Repair Garage on Winslow and Harrison, just three blocks away. It was the first time Daddy had been home for dinner in a long while and I didn't want our time together spoiled by an argument.

But my parents wouldn't let it go. Between passing the mashed potatoes and gravy, Daddy fired back. "Winning is not always the most important end. Being a good friend is just as important, Rosemary." He was talking to me, but looking at Mama.

Mama stopped eating and pushed away from the table. She shot back with, "But first, Rosemary needs to be a good friend to herself." It became a ping-pong of words and I was the spectator, looking from one to the other.

Daddy stopped eating, too, and leaned back. He folded his arms. "Women need to be supportive of their men, not combative."

"Women need to be able to use their skills to be as good as they can be. So what if she's smarter? So what if she makes more money? If she's good at something, then so be it." Mama tossed her napkin on the table and walked to the sink.

Daddy shoved his plate forward, half of his dinner still left. "I don't want my daughter growing up with weird ideas like . . ."

"Mine?" Mama interrupted angrily.

For sure, Mama and Daddy weren't talking about my promise to J.J. anymore.

Daddy threw up his arms and let them fall to each side. Unable to gather his thoughts, he left in a huff.

"You always walk away instead of talking things through," Mama yelled. I heard Daddy's truck speed out of the driveway.

I tried thinking of a happier time, before he opened his shop. He used to be a Universal Life Insurance agent. And before that, Mama and Daddy lived in Memphis, Tennessee. I was born there, but I don't remember anything about it. We moved to Kirkland, Missouri — just outside St. Louis — when I was two years old. We were happy when Daddy finally opened his shop. Mama is a seamstress who makes clothes for people all over the city. She took pride in hand-stitching "Mel Patterson — Owner" on three of Daddy's blue shop shirts. He was equally as proud to wear them. I wonder, now, where all that happiness has gone.

Suddenly, J.J. nudges me, bringing me back to the present. "Here they come," he says between clenched teeth.

I know who he means instantly. And I brace for what I know is headed our way.

The five Hamilton kids. They taught the Wicked Witch of the East how to be mean and ornery to the Munchkins of Oz. Their family moved from Arkansas to Kirkland late last year, and they've made quite a name for themselves. In fact, if the Ku Klux Klan and the notorious Al Capone and the whole Chicago mob were bearing down on us, it wouldn't be any worse than facing the Hamiltons.

I've given each one a gangster name based on my favorite radio series, *Gang Busters*. There's Curl-lipped Jane, the oldest, who is about seventeen. She's flanked by her brothers, Stevie the Snake and Wayne the Whiner. They're fifteen and sixteen. Snot-nosed Marty who is twelve and Grace the Tasteless take up the rear.

Grace, the youngest of the clan, makes eye contact with me. I hold her in my gaze until she looks away. First time I've gotten her to blink. Our backyards are joined, but we don't go to the same school. We don't play in the same places. We've not been to each other's houses, and I can't imagine the two of us ever sharing a secret.

The Hamiltons push past us and go into Mr. Bob's store. J.J. and I watch them the way one might watch a number of rattlesnakes — fascinated, but terrified of what they're capable of doing. "I wish they'd stayed in Arkansas," J.J. whispers.

I wish it, too, but the reality is they live in Kirkland now.

Their house is on Kaye Lane, but everybody calls it Dead End because of the big Dead End sign positioned at the entrance to their street. Ask anybody in Kirkland where Kaye Lane is and odds are they won't know. Ask where Dead End is and everybody knows that's where six white families live surrounded by colored people. Most of the people who live on Dead End are decent, hardworking people, trying to raise their families, same as anybody else. They don't bother us and we don't bother them.

But the Hamiltons came and now things are different. They pick fights and call us names all the time. They hate colored people and don't mind telling us.

As usual, the kids come out of the store with a bunch of junk — bags of potato chips, soda, candy, and gum. What a gross breakfast.

Stevie the Snake bumps up against me. "Move outta my way!"

I shove him back.

Just then, Bevvy comes out of the store. All she has to do is give them a look. Nobody messes with Bevvy.

One day, after the Hamiltons had bombarded J.J. and me with rocks and every ugly word in their vocabulary, Bevvy stepped in with a few choice words of her own and ran them off. Then Bevvy gave J.J. and me a fast lesson in self-defense. "I'm not always going to be around to help. So you need to learn how to defend yourselves. Just remember, their bark is fierce, but their bite is weak. Fight back and they'll leave you alone."

The next time one of the Hamiltons said something ornery, we hit back with a few hard words of our own. The Hamiltons' attacks slackened. But they haven't stopped.

As we move away, Grace the Tasteless sticks out her tongue at me and I shake my fist at her. War talk. But no battle will ensue this morning. Bevvy leads us away and Curl-lipped Jane leads her motley crew in the opposite direction.

■   ■   ■

So here I am on the last day of school — the last day for Attucks Elementary, ever.

J.J. and I run to the corner. I'm careful not to make it seem like a race, but I pull ahead just to prove I could beat him easily, if I tried.

The three of us turn the familiar corner at Milwaukee and Ranger streets. Attucks Elementary School sits comfortably among old oak and elm trees. The cornerstone reads, *"Attucks School — Grades K through 12."* It was completed way back in 1925 "for the colored children of Kirkland, Missouri." Built the same year Mama was born, twenty-nine years ago. It's too soon for it to be closed. Surely they won't tear it down, but what will they do with the building, if it isn't a school?

We pause to speak to Mr. Beavers, the custodian, not just to say good-bye for the summer, but forever. He is out front, planting petunias and marigolds around the school sign. Why? I wonder. He waves and we wave back.

Bevvy heads for the high school section and J.J. and I bound up the steps of the lower school building, and stop. I hold the door a little longer and let myself ease through the opening slowly. It is the last time I will do any of this again.

CHAPTER TWO

School's Out

Same Day

The wooden plaque sits in the middle of our teacher's desk.

Mrs. V. Washington, Fifth Grade
Attucks Elementary School, Kirkland, Missouri
1953–54

It's been on her desk since the first day of school back in September. I remember when she told us her son had made the plaque in his shop class. Mrs. Washington is the best teacher in the school. But it's not just my opinion. All forty-one of her students in 5A think so. What's not to like? She's smart and nice, but not a pushover. She's tough and won't put up with nonsense, but she's always fair. That's the best part about her.

The V in her name stands for Vanessa, but I wouldn't dream of speaking a teacher's first name out loud — especially Mrs. Washington. The idea makes my toes tingle. But one day on a bet, Avon James stood in the playground and yelled "VANESSA" at the top of his lungs. We all waited for a hand to burst through the clouds and crush him like an egg, but Avon lives. And to this day, he has an honored place in our class. He alone said the teacher's first name and got away with it. None of us — not even J.J. — has ever been that daring.

Next to Mrs. Washington's plaque is a box, neatly wrapped in the school colors — bright blue paper with a red bow.

"Open your gift, Mrs. Washington," says Kevin, the class treasurer. It is the custom at Attucks for all the classes to give their teachers gifts at the end of the school year. We don't have to, but we like doing it. I remember we gave our kindergarten teacher a set of four teacups and saucers; first grade was an umbrella; second grade was garden tools, and so on.

This year, Kevin collected a dime from each of us — every single person contributed — and it was enough for Kevin's mother to special-order our gift.

Mrs. Washington opens the box. When she sees it, she covers her face.

"It must be something awful," whispers one of the boys.

"What did you buy?" Clyde asks, sounding real disgusted.

"You just wait and see," says Kevin, sounding confident.

"No, no, no," says Mrs. Washington, holding up her hand. She shows us a coffee cup with the words: *The Best Teacher Ever*. We all ooh and ah. "I don't like it," says Mrs. Washington. Somebody gasps. "I love it!" Then everybody starts clapping.

"See what I told you," says Kevin, sticking out his chest. He's relieved. So am I. I let myself breathe a sign of relief, because I'm the class president. And if the gift had been bad, the class would have never let me forget it.

"I will keep this thoughtful gift and each time I drink a cup of coffee or tea or my favorite hot chocolate, I'll think of this year's fifth-grade class and smile."

Ahhhhhh! The girls sigh. "That's so sweet."

"Mrs. Washington," Estelean blurts out, breaking the magic of the moment. "Is it true? Are you going to move down south?" Estelean reminds me of a squirrel wearing glasses. Her movements are quick and jittery. But she is my best friend of all the girls. I help her with her writing, and she helps me with my math.

"It is no secret. I am going to Nashville, Tennessee, to work on my Masters in Education," Mrs. Washington answers.

"Didn't you already go to college?" Arthur Lee asks.

"Yes. But I'm going back to school so that I can learn how to become a better teacher, Gabe."

I smile, remembering Arthur Lee as Gabriel in the Christmas play. He forgot his lines. So his mother whispered them from the audience. We've been calling him Gabe ever since — even Mrs. Washington calls him Gabe.

"You're already the best teacher in the world," Charley puts in.

"That's the most sense you've made all year," J.J. whispers. Everybody giggles.

"Too bad the report cards are already made out, J.J.," Charley says with a smirk. He and J.J. are very competitive. One is always trying to outdo the other.

Mrs. Washington tells us a little about what she is going to be doing in the fall. "I'll be studying under one of the most knowledgeable professors in elementary education," she says. It sounds so important — so teacher-like. "A lot of opportunities will be opening up for your generation, for all people of color."

"Why is the school board closing Attucks and making us go to their schools? Doesn't make sense to me," I say. Heads nod in agreement.

Mrs. Washington holds up her hand. "That's not good thinking. Public schools belong to all of us. If white and black children study, play, and grow up together, they will learn to respect all citizens regardless of race, color, or religion. And the world will be a better place."

That sounds so teachery, like she memorized it the way we had to memorize "The Creation" by James Weldon Johnson. I like Mrs. Washington, but she can't convince me that a school full of white kids and teachers belongs to me.

Suddenly, J.J. leaps out of his seat, waving his hand. He usually gets into trouble for that, but not today. Today is special. "Mrs. Washington, I was thinking. . . ." he says.

"Thought I smelled something burning," Charley whispers.

J.J. is too excited to care about the smart remark. "Why don't you stay here in Kirkland and start your very own school, and then we can be your students? And then you can teach us all that good stuff. We could even let a few white kids in. And then . . . and then. . . ." J.J. is breathless with excitement. "And then . . . that's all. What do you think?" He looks around, takes a bow, and sits down. A few heads are bobbing, but one look at Mrs. Washington's expression and we know that J.J.'s idea is not going to fly.

"I'm deeply moved," she says. "My, oh my. I'd never thought of opening my own school. I'm afraid that's out of the question. But nothing would please me more than to have a school full of children just as smart, creative, talented, and inquisitive as you have been this year."

Mrs. Washington moves to the front of her desk and leans against it. "Now it is time to move on," she says. "But no matter what happens in the future, I want you to hold your head up, speak clearly, and do your best. Promise me that."

"We promise," we answer.

"We won't ever forget you," says Li'l Bit. Her real name is Flora. We call her Li'l Bit 'cause she's so tiny. Although she is small, what she just said is large. I won't forget Mrs. Vanessa Washington, the best teacher ever.

Now it's time to get our report cards.

Why is it that the kids who get the best grades always act like they're terrified of seeing their report cards? We line up. Marian

Ambry, one of the best students in fifth grade, is wringing her hands and hopping from foot to foot like she's got something to worry about.

Now J.J., that's another story. He's got plenty to be concerned about. I glance back at him. He's looking pitiful.

I feel I've done well in everything except math. Math is my worst subject, but I'm hoping the grade isn't below a C.

After we've cleaned out our desks, Mrs. Washington begins calling names in alphabetical order. "Ashcraft, Awell," she calls and explains. "Inside your grades you'll see what school you've been assigned to next year." As each student steps up, Mrs. Washington says a personal good-bye. "Benton, Brooks, Carson, and Davis . . . Estelean you are very good in math and science. One day, I wouldn't be a bit surprised if you helped us reach the moon."

Estelean just grins, same as the Cheshire Cat.

Finally, Mrs. Washington comes to me. "Patterson."

I'm suddenly overcome with emotion and I hug my teacher around the waist. Other girls have hugged Mrs. Washington all year, but I never have. She's startled at first, but I feel her relax into the hug and she squeezes me. "Rosemary, you're a scholar and an athlete," she says. "That's a winning combination. You've been a great class president with outstanding leadership skills. Who knows, one day you might run for president of the United States. And I will be the first to vote for you."

My mouth drops. Me? The president? I am so flattered, it's

embarrassing. I don't know what to say, so I just stand there with a stupid grin on my face.

"I'll be expecting great things from you one day," Mrs. Washington adds, all the time smiling.

I thank her, then grab a quick glimpse at my card. All A's. Even in math. I hug Mrs. Washington one more time, and step aside before I make a bigger fool of myself.

There is also an official-looking letter inside the envelope. I've been assigned to Robertson Elementary for fall term 1954–55. The space for the teacher's name is filled in with "unknown."

"I'm going to Adams," says Estelean. "That's not fair, separating us."

I am saddened by that, but then I remember. "Estelean, we live two blocks apart. We'll still see each other."

"But not every day." She heads for home, but I wait for J.J.

I'm thinking, *Nobody seems to be assigned to Robertson.* It's hard to imagine being in a new school without any of my friends. *Why am I worried?* I ask myself.

"Stenson," Mrs. Washington calls. J.J. steps up, head down, face looking like he's lost his best friend. Mama argues that J.J. only has himself to blame for not having good grades. Daddy, on the other hand, says not everybody can make straight A's.

"What J.J. lacks in the classroom, he makes up for in the garage," says Daddy. "That boy is only ten, but he's as smart as a whip when it comes to fixing machines."

That may be true. But right now, fixing machines is not what's going to get J.J. passed to sixth grade. What he needs is a miracle.

"What did I tell you about your head?" Mrs. Washington says sternly. "Hold your head up, even though we both know why you're looking pitiful. You can do better than this," she says, giving him his report card and adding, "There is no reason why you couldn't be an A student. You need to settle down and take your lessons more seriously."

"Yes, ma'am," he answers.

"You're really a bright kid, J.J.," Mrs. Washington says, softening her tone. She pats him on the back. "Good luck."

J.J. and I don't talk until we've said good-bye to everything and everybody in the school. This isn't the normal end of a school year. It is the end of our *school*. For me, it is a sad time, but as far as I can see, most of the grown-ups seem to be happy about it.

"It's going to be so much better for you next year," says our principal, Mr. Porter. He's been assigned to be the assistant principal at Kirkland High School. *Are white schools that much better than ours?* I wonder.

"Good-bye, Mr. Beavers," I call.

"Why are you planting flowers if they're going to close the school?" J.J. asks.

"I'll keep the ol' place pretty as long as I can. Hard to break old habits." And he waves his hat. "Have a good summer."

Once we pass the Attucks sign, we are officially off Attucks campus. "School's out. School's out. The teacher wore her shoes out," J.J. and I skip and sing. There are many versions of the chant, but some of them I won't sing. Somebody might hear me and tell Mama. Then I'm in trouble. Which means no radio shows. So, "School's out. School's out. The teacher wore her shoes out" is as daring as I'm willing to get.

J.J. asks what my grades are. I tell him all A's. "You must be some kind of genius," he says, making me sound like I'm an alien from Mars or beyond the Milky Way.

"No, I just work hard and do my homework." Then I tell him what Mrs. Washington said about me being president.

"President! On the planet Zylon, maybe," he says. "A girl can't be president — and a colored girl at that. Mrs. Washington knows better."

My wonderful bubble bursts. J.J. is right — never in a million years could I be president. But seeing myself as president had been fun, if only for a moment. "I don't want to be president anyway. I want to be a writer when I grow up. Work for a newspaper or maybe write books. That's my real dream." Nothing could be better than writing dramas for my favorite radio show, *Gang Busters*.

"I hate writing," J.J. says softy. "But hey, will you put me in one of your stories? Maybe they'll make a movie out of it and I'll be famous."

"For sure, and your gangster name will be Jumping Jack Stenson in a Stetson hat. Or maybe you want to be a G-man. What will it be?"

"I haven't decided yet," J.J. says, managing a weak smile.

He hasn't opened his report card. So I take a chance and encourage him. "Go on. Look at your grades. It is what it is. Get it over with."

J.J. shrugs. "I don't care what my grades are."

Of course he does. "Want me to look for you?"

J.J. hands me his card without a fuss. I open it. A part of me wants to tease him and make him suffer for giving me such a hard time. But this is not joking time. J.J. might keel over if he thinks he's failed.

"You passed," I say. "Your grades are awful — mostly C's and D's, but you made enough to pass on to sixth grade." But what really makes me happiest is that he's been assigned to Robertson, too. "We're going to the same school next year."

"I passed! I passed!" That is all J.J. needs to know. With a whoop and a holler he takes off down the street, yelling at the top of his voice. "School's out! School's out! The teacher wore her shoes out."

"School's out! School's out!" I sing. The promises I made are over now! I can finally race J.J. without holding back. So I pull up beside him with ease. We're neck and neck. Then I kick it up a notch and pass him.

"You're part rabbit, girl," he says, bent over breathlessly.

Standing at the top of Ranger Street, I look back at Attucks and utter a quiet good-bye. School is out.

CHAPTER THREE

In Need of Help

Later, Same Day

As is the tradition, J.J. and I stop by Mr. Bob's Grocery Store to show our report cards. Bevvy is there, too.

"Well, well, well, look at this," says Mr. Bob, admiring my grades. "This is mighty nice." Then, opening Bevvy's grades, he smiles. "So you're a big-time senior," he says. "Congratulations!"

Bevvy is beaming. "I'm going to secretarial school when I finish high school."

Then when Mr. Bob opens J.J.'s card, he frowns. "Boy, you can do better than this!"

"But I passed to sixth grade," J.J. says with a slight whine.

"Barely," says Mr. Bob, sternly. "Come next year, you won't be able to mess around, young man. You're going to the white school, so you'll have to apply yourself. Work hard! Study! Make us proud."

J.J. nods. "That's next year. Right now, I'm happy I passed

and school is out for the summer," he says, trying to hide his embarrassment.

Mr. Bob shakes his head. "What will we do with you, J.J. Stenson? Well, since you all passed, pick out a treat."

Bevvy chooses a dill pickle. Then, figuring J.J. and I can get home from Mr. Bob's safely, she hurries to meet her boyfriend, Tommy Lee. I choose a PayDay, my favorite candy bar. It takes J.J. a century to choose, because he likes everything. I leave him to make his decision alone.

"Later."

"'Gator."

As usual, I use the shortcut down the Frisco railroad tracks toward Daddy's garage. It's fun to walk on the steel beams, pretending I'm a tightrope walker in the circus. Meanwhile, my mind is running at full speed, thinking about what Robertson Elementary will be like next year. Will the kids be nice? Is "unknown" going to be a good teacher? Will she like me? What if my teacher is a he? Then I decide to be more like J.J. I won't waste a minute more worrying about *what-ifs*. Let September come. I'm going to enjoy my summer.

Then I see it.

I've seen plenty of dead things on the railroad tracks before — raccoons, squirrels, a possum or two. Cold, stiff, lifeless little creatures. All dead. But I've never seen anything like the critter lying at my feet. It looks like somebody's black, brown-and-white, oily, and bloody fur coat.

I was six when I saw death up close and personal, when Happy, my parakeet, died. Daddy explained that everything living has to die. "It is the way the world is ordered. Living creatures are born. They live. They die." He'd told me the same thing when Big Papa died a year later.

"It was Big Papa's time to be with Happy," I remember saying. I was trying very hard to show Daddy what a big girl I was, and that I could handle a grown-up idea.

"Nothing fearful about death," Daddy answered, nodding his head. "But we should live our lives so that when our time comes, the world won't owe us a thing."

I didn't get it. What would the world owe him and why? Daddy always says I'll understand when I'm older. I am older — older than I was then — but I still don't get it.

I'm wondering what this creature might have been before it was so horribly twisted and mangled? Surely the world owed it a better way to die. It doesn't have the markings of a raccoon or a possum. I decide that it's probably a cat. "It was your time," I whisper.

Suddenly the cat moves.

Startled, I stumble backward, almost falling. The cat is still alive. I reach out, but withdraw my hand quickly because I know better than to touch a wounded animal. Daddy has often warned me never to go near a critter that's hurt. "Animals who are in pain will sometimes attack the one who's trying to help them. Besides it might be rabid, and you don't want those shots in your navel, do you?"

Mama shushed Daddy, saying he was overdoing it, especially when he described the gruesome details of rabies shots. But it is that fear that is keeping me honest when it comes to touching *this* poor cat.

I move in closer. The creature is breathing in short gurgling gasps. Blood trickles out of its mouth. Part of its ear is hanging to the side like a piece of torn material. Can it hear me? The cat moves again — a hopping, flopping motion. My mind is spinning with questions. What if it's not the cat's time to die? Could I help it? I take off running, yelling for Daddy. He'll know what to do.

"Help! Daddy, Daddy, Daddy!" I turn the corner, head down, feet churning at full speed. I pass Mr. Logan, who works for Daddy. He's rotating tires on Mr. Beaver's '51 Chevy. Before I reach Daddy's office, he's already run out to meet me. I fall into his arms.

"Wait. Hold on! Hold on! Tell me, what is it?" Daddy looks over my shoulder to see what I'm running from.

"It's a cat . . . all broken upon the railroad tracks. Come see." I'm breathless, but I keep on talking. "It's still breathing. . . ."

"A cat?" says Mr. Logan, blowing air through his teeth. "I

thought a panther was after you, girl." Mr. Logan chuckles and goes back to work.

"A cat!" Daddy throws his arms in the air the way he does when he can't find words to fit his feelings; then his arms flop to his sides the way he does when he's found the words, but isn't sure he should say them. He sighs deeply. "Rosemary, you scared me to death with all that commotion. You are too excitable — just like Doris. I thought the worst."

Daddy always says I'm like Mama when I do something he doesn't like. She always says I'm just like him when I get on her nerves. Trouble is, they both want to claim me when I do well.

Right now, I don't care who I'm like. "Come quick! It's a cat on the railroad tracks. It's hurt awful bad, but it's alive. You have to come see, 'cause I can't touch it unless you are with me. It needs help . . . and . . ."

"Hold on, Rosemary!" Daddy says. "I've got things to do, honey. If a train has hit the cat, it's dead, even if it's still breathing. So let the poor critter stay where it is and die in peace."

"You said cats have 9 lives." I remind him of what he's told me many times. "Maybe this is only life number 4 or 5 — or even 8 — but not 9."

Daddy flashes one of his teasing smiles. "It's amazing how you remember everything I say, when it's convenient for you to remember. Like I told you, baby girl, I have work to do.

"Daddy, please. The cat needs your help. We need your help. . . ." I plead. Daddy lets me get away with far more than Mama does, but I'm pushing his patience right now and I know it.

"Let it go, Rosemary," he says seriously. "I have a pickup at 4 o'clock."

Just then, I hear a woman's voice from Daddy's office. "Melvin, you've got time before your 4 o'clock pickup to see what Rosie is talking about." Nobody in the world calls me Rosie, and nobody calls my father Melvin. He's just plain Mel Patterson.

A young woman, totally overdressed for an auto garage, steps into the shop area where we're talking. Jean Casey. She's been Daddy's secretary and office manager since Mama quit a year ago to pursue her sewing business.

When Daddy started the shop there was only Mr. Logan, who is a top-notch mechanic, Mama, and me. I can see myself coloring on the office floor while Mama answered the calls, arranged the appointments, kept the books, and made the bank deposits. But then Mama wanted to start making more clothes for people, to expand her business. Daddy didn't like it. "I don't want my wife working. It looks as though I can't take care of my family without your help," I heard Daddy argue.

"Why worry about what others are thinking?" she replied.

"I need you to help me."

"And I could use a word of encouragement from you."

Mama began sewing full-time, and Daddy hired Miss Jean to take on Mama's responsibilities at the shop.

To me, that woman's as fake as a Halloween false face. If I could peel away the makeup and rouge, I'd find a horror underneath. Even though she tries to be nice, there's something about her that irks me. Why can't she just be nice, rather than try to be what she thinks is nice?

To make matters worse, Miss Jean giggles. Can you imagine a grown woman giggling? The sound is weird.

"Hi, Rosie," Miss Jean says as she gingerly tiptoes in high-heeled shoes around an oil spot. "Oooo. Yuk."

"Hello, Miss Jean." I speak politely, but I want to yell that my name is Rosemary and not Rosie. She's the only person who calls me Rosie, in a deep, nail-dragging, southern drawl. She came here from Louisville, Kentucky, a few years back. Tall, heart-stopping pretty, young, and very shapely, like the girls in the centerfold of *Jet* magazine. "Don't worry, Rosie. I'll get your Daddy to change his mind."

"Thank you, Miss *Jeannie*," I say, imitating her accent. I hope she gets my point.

Meanwhile, she steps over another oil spot and pulls Daddy to the side. I can't really hear what she's saying, but Daddy's attitude changes immediately. "Okay," he says, smiling broadly again. "It's two against one. I'll go see about the beastie you're talking about, Rosie."

"Rosemary!" I snap at him. "You named me Rosemary Elizabeth Patterson after my grandmothers. Your mama hates the name Rosie and so do I." I'm talking to Daddy but looking at Miss Jean. I am dangerously close to being sassy. But Daddy knows how touchy I am about my name. So he lets it slide.

"Okay, okay," Daddy says, holding up his hands as if to ward off a cold blast of wind. He quickly finds a box and throws some rags in it.

"Show me," he says.

Without saying a word, I run ahead, hoping the cat is not dead.

Back at the tracks, we find the cat lying in a heap. Daddy's eyes show his concern. He shakes his head. "The cat is dead, honey."

My eyes fill with tears. "No! Daddy, it's still breathing. See?"

"Maybe. But that's not living. It would be more merciful if the creature died. At least then it won't be suffering."

Tears meander down my face even though I try to hold them back.

Daddy wipes away a tear on my chin. "I don't want to raise your hopes. The cat will be dead before morning, baby girl. Understand that?"

I nod my head, but my heart is breaking.

Thinking for a moment, Daddy says kindly, "What do you want me to do?"

"I want you to help it," I whisper.

"All I can do is make it comfortable until . . ."

"That's enough," I say between sniffs.

Daddy uses his heavy gloves to gently roll the wounded cat into the box. It lets out a shrill groan that sounds both horrifying and pitiful at the same time. It makes me so sad, I cry hot, salty tears all the way back to the garage.

"Let's put a bowl of water down for it," I plead.

"Rosemary," Daddy says in his best no-nonsense voice, "We've done all we can. Its wounds are too severe. The cat is suffering." Daddy bends down on one knee and pulls me into the circle of his large arms. I rest my head on his shoulder as he whispers, "It wouldn't have much of a life even if it lives. Its body is so badly crippled. I need you to accept that the cat will die. What you are doing is humane. We are making it comfortable in its final hours."

Realizing he is right, I swallow to choke back another round of tears. "I know, Daddy."

"That's my girl," he says. "You're a real Patterson. Got your feet planted squarely on the ground." A little while ago, I was excitable like Mama. Now I'm solid like a Patterson.

Back at the office, Daddy puts the cat in the box in a corner of the shop. Then he takes his keys off the board and beckons for Miss Jean to follow. Usually, Mr. Logan or Daddy goes for a pickup in the truck with big black and red letters that read: MEL'S ABLE AUTO REPAIR GARAGE. Today, Daddy and Miss Jean leave in *her* car. For a pickup?

One look at them together and I realize the awful truth.

"Rosemary," Daddy calls. "Tell your mother I have to work late."

"What about the cat?"

"Leave the box in the corner there. We'll take care of it in the morning."

As they drive away, I call to Daddy. "I forgot to tell you, I got all A's on my report card and I passed to sixth grade."

He stops the car, holds out his arm, and makes an "O" with his pointer finger and thumb. I smile because that means I've done very well and he's pleased. "I'll be going to Robertson in . . ."

But before I can finish he has sped away.

I feel for sure now that Miss Jean is the reason why Daddy doesn't come home. She's why Mama cries so much. She's why they argue all the time. "Miss Jean is a horrible woman, hiding behind a mask," I mumble to myself.

I don't hear J.J. come up behind me on his bicycle until he speaks. "They tell me addled people talk to themselves." He shakes his head pathetically.

"Naw." I disagree. "Only when we answer ourselves is there a problem."

J.J. shrugs. "Whatever. You sure sound angry. Something wrong?"

"Hey, I'm not mad," I say, trying to hide my feelings. I think J.J. suspects that things are not all that good with my folks. No telling what he's overheard. But he never asks and I keep my feelings to myself.

In a more cheerful voice, I draw J.J.'s attention away from my worries. "Bet you'll never guess what's in this box."

"A pair of your stinky shoes," he replies, teasing, but all the time going over to see what's in the box. One look and J.J. makes a gagging sound. "Ugh! What is it?"

"It's a cat. I found it on the railroad tracks!" Seeing that J.J. is really interested, I rush on, explaining, "Daddy put it in this box full of rags so it will be comfortable until it dies. Poor thing probably won't last until morning."

"But what will you do if it's alive in the morning?" J.J. asks.

The idea of the cat living hasn't been a consideration, because Daddy's so sure that it will die. "I don't know."

J.J. looks past my shoulder. I can tell by the expression on his face that one of the Dead End kids is coming our way.

J.J. and I watch in amazement as all five Hamiltons approach. It makes me crazy mad when they come to buy soda from Daddy's machine. If they had a machine, they wouldn't let me come near it. But Daddy won't stop the Hamiltons from buying soda, no matter how much I complain. "Long as they pay, baby girl, I don't care."

Jane drops in two dimes, then slides and pulls two frosty bottles of Coca-Cola from the chest. She pops the caps and hands a bottle to Grace. She gives the other bottle to Stevie, who swallows a big gulp then passes it to Wayne.

"Blah! Nasty," says J.J., twisting his face. "You couldn't pay me to drink after my brothers. All that slobbery juice running back into the bottle. Nasty."

"I don't think it's all that bad," I say, thinking I might enjoy sharing a soda with a sister or brother. In an odd way, I envy the Hamiltons. They're a big family and even though they're as mean as hornets, they seem to get along with one another very well.

They sure look alike. Each has the same narrow face and winter blue eyes. The two oldest boys resemble Mr. Hamilton, who is a big red-faced man, short and stocky in build. I see him walking to the bus stop every morning on his way to work at Scullins Steel Company. He always carries a black, round-top lunch pail under his arm and a newspaper. But his head is always down as if he's deep in thought. I've never known him to speak to anybody. I can't help but think how different he is from Daddy, who is tall and slender and talks all the time, always ready to share a funny story.

The girls are a spitting image of their mother. Mrs. Hamilton looks like all the other Dead End women — plain, ordinary, almost like a sheet of typing paper. Neutral. When I see her in Mr. Bob's Grocery Store now and then with Jane or Grace, I can tell she would rather be shopping somewhere else. Most of the time the Dead End women walk to Krogers uptown rather than shop at Mr. Bob's. "But when they need to put something on credit, they shop at Mr. Bob's fast enough," Mama told Aunt Betty. I wasn't supposed to hear, but I did.

I remember one day noticing Mrs. Hamilton's long, slender fingers with a single gold band on her left hand — same as Mama. But unlike Mama, there is nothing slender or graceful about the rest of Mrs. Hamilton. She's a big woman as round as she is tall with a mop of curly black hair. If Mr. Hamilton is a grizzly, then Mrs. Hamilton is a bear in her own right.

Stevie, the one who looks the most like his father, sucks down the last of the pop. His brothers protest. I wonder again what it must be like to have a brother or sister to share with, run with, and even fuss with. J.J.'s the closest I've got to a sibling. The idea of being related to four or five other James Johnson Stensons — all living in the same house at the same time — makes me dismiss that idea right away.

"What's in the box?" Stevie the Snake asks, walking over to see for himself. After one look, he scoffs. "Hey, look, they got a dead cat in here."

"It's not dead," I shout.

Grace the Tasteless comes over to see. "What'd you do to it?" she asks, as if we were responsible for the cat's condition.

"It's none of your business," I say with my hands on my hips. "But just so you know, we found the cat on the railroad tracks. And we're decent enough to make it comfortable while it's dying," I explain, adding, "so there!"

J.J. doesn't add to the conversation. He's all the time giving the Hamiltons an unblinking stare.

"You'd better stop eyeballing us or else," Marty sneers. His voice is a rattlesnake's warning.

I have no doubt from past experiences that the Hamiltons usually make good on their threats. But J.J. isn't one to back down from a challenge and neither am I.

"We ain't looking at *nothing*," J.J. says, emphasizing each sylla-ble of the word to make sure it's understood to be an insult. My fists are balled and ready for battle. "Rosemary, didn't your daddy empty the *trash* today?" J.J. asks me. It is my cue.

"No, he forgot to sweep up the *trash* and throw it out!" My conduct would *not* make my mother happy. To be honest, I don't enjoy being hateful, but it's the only thing the Hamiltons understand.

Truth is, if they weren't so mean, I'd feel sorry for them. They don't have any more than we do, yet they think of themselves as better off than us because they're white. Talk about dumb.

Time and time again Mama's told me to ignore them. "They are sad, unhappy, small-minded people," she explains. "They use name-calling to make themselves feel bigger and better than you."

Daddy had even talked to J.J. and me about it. "Don't allow words to cripple your spirits. You are as good as anybody, and I don't want you to ever think differently."

I don't know how J.J. feels, but words do hurt.

Curl-lipped Jane takes the last swallow from her bottle and places it in the case. "No deposit," she says with a scowl. "I hear y'all are gonna be coming to *our* school next year."

"I didn't know the Hamiltons owned a school," J.J. says.

"You know what she means," Grace puts in. "They're closing the colored school, so y'all will be coming to our school."

"So what?" I say, stepping forward. "Robertson is a brand-new school — belongs to you and belongs to us, too. And J.J. and I, we're gonna show you a thing or two when we get there."

"There are more of us than there are of you. So don't nothing belong to you," Stevie put in.

"Public schools belong to all of us," I say. "There's no such thing as white or colored schools. Put that in your nose and smell it."

Snot-nosed Marty steps up. "Why don't you go on back to Africa?"

Jane waves them off. Then they disappear around the side of the garage. Grace the Tasteless pokes out her tongue. Of all the Hamiltons, she's the one I dislike the most.

They're gone. Good.

J.J. returns to the box where the wounded cat is lying still and quiet. "What's its name?" he asks.

"I just found it on the railroad tracks after school let out. Why would I name a dying cat?"

J.J. absently puts a dime in the soda machine and buys a cola. His mind is not on what he's doing. He looks thoughtful, a rare moment. After taking a big sip, J.J. wipes his mouth with the back of his arm and belches. "'Scuse me," he says, adding quickly, "it looks like a lot of rags. Why don't we call him Rags?"

"We?" It's just like J.J. to claim ownership of a cat I found.

"Yeah, *we*," he answers. "You've given up on him. I haven't, so I'm claiming the half that lives. The part that dies is your half."

Baloney! But I'm thinking there is no need to argue over the ownership of an almost-dead cat.

"Rags sounds like a boy's name. How do you know it's a boy cat?"

"'Cause! A girl cat would have been dead," he says with certainty. "Besides," he continues, "Rags fits a boy or girl." He tenderly reaches in to rub its matted fur. The cat lets out a yelp of painful protest.

J.J. rests his head in his palms. "He'll make it if he fights. So I'm not giving up on you. You're going to live," he whispers to the pile of misshapen fur.

"Poor Rags," I whisper, then pause. I've just called the cat by a name . . . not "it" or "critter" or "thing." Rags. I've named a dying cat Rags, as though he's my beloved pet.

The next morning, Rags is still alive. He's clinging to life and won't let go, though I can hardly call it *living*. His body is so broken, but he's still breathing — each gasp a pain-filled labor.

Then at breakfast Daddy says, "It's a miracle." He shakes his head and I see a little twinkle in his eye, telling me he's getting ready to tease. "That critter is still living and J.J. got promoted to sixth grade. Why it's enough to make a believer out of me," he says laughing. And at the same time, he passes me the jelly.

"Oh, Daddy, don't be so hard on J.J.," I say, and pass him butter for his biscuits.

"At least I got you to smile."

"Please, Daddy, may I bring the cat home?"

"Ask your mama," he says, ducking the responsibility.

"The cat needs to be taken to a vet," Mama says between clenched teeth. "In fact, it should have been taken as soon as it was found. An idiot would have known to do it."

"That's it," Daddy says, throwing his arms in the air. He sighs and pushes back in his chair. Then his arms flop to his sides. "How dare you call me an idiot in front of my daughter?"

Mama's eyes flash dark. "If the shoe fits, wear it. Rosemary finds a cat on the railroad tracks and you let her get attached to it without taking it to a vet?"

"The cat looked like it was going to die," Daddy shoots back defensively. "I never expected the thing to live. I think it's stupid to waste money taking a half-dead cat to a vet."

Mama gasps. "Now you're calling me stupid, like a little name-calling boy!"

"Who're you calling a little boy?"

I can't take any more of their fighting. "Stop! Stop! Stop!" I shout, while covering my ears. "You both are stupid for fighting."

The sound of my words hang in the room like an ugly picture. Mama and Daddy are speechless. I try to wish away the moment, but it lingers. So I run to my room to escape.

I stay in my room most of the morning, trying not to call too much attention to myself. Daddy leaves, but at noon he comes back to the house with Rags loaded in the truck. He seems calmer now, less angry. I'm all the time holding my breath, hoping he isn't mad at me for what I said. When I see Daddy, I go to the porch. Mama joins me. She is still angry. I can hear anger in her shallow breathing. I can feel anger in the way her arms are folded across her body. Then I see her dark, dark eyes and it pains me to think that I might be the cause of her feelings.

"Mama, I'm so sorry. Please don't be upset with me."

She squeezes my hand. "Go see about your cat," she says with a kiss on my forehead. Then she goes back into the house before her eyes spill over.

"Hop in," Daddy says. "We'll take the cat to the vet and we'll see what happens from there."

"His name is Rags," I say. As we pull away I see Mama standing by the window. There is no anger in her face now, only sadness.

"Rags? The name fits." Daddy laughs as we pull away.

J.J. is sitting on my front porch, waiting patiently to get the news, when Daddy and I return from the vet's office. I jump out of the car, talking. "Rags is going to make it," I shout. "Dr. Jacobi says that it's going to take a long, long time to heal. But isn't that good news?"

"I told you!" he says, doing a cartwheel flip. "You need to listen to me, girl. I am the great Marvellini. I can see into the future." He struts around with his thumbs tucked under his armpits, imitating the voice of the radio character we love so much.

"Well, Great Marvellini, you missed that Rags is a she-cat," I say, with my hands on my hips. "Yes, Rags is a girl!"

"Gosh. Rags is a girl," J.J. repeats my words, smiling. He's determined to have the last word. "Well, the Great Marvellini knew the cat was either a boy or a girl. So at least the name still fits."

Baloney!

J.J. listens while I give him Dr. Jacobi's full report. "Even though the doctor had to stitch up a huge gash in Rags's side, none of her vital organs are injured."

"She looks so broken laying in that box," says J.J.

"It *is* sad," I agree. "She lost an eye, an ear, and a hind leg. But Dr. Jacobi says if she gets good care and lots of love, she will heal and live a good while."

We sit on the porch and listen to *Our Gal Sunday*, while we keep watch over Rags as she sleeps off the anesthesia.

"What do you want to be when you grow up?" I ask J.J. "I've never heard you say."

He shrugs.

"You'd make a good veterinarian."

"Yeah, that sounds good. I like it," he says.

"Then you'll have to start doing better in school. You can't keep messing around. Especially next year at the white school."

"See, there you go again!" J.J. sounds put off.

"Hey, all I'm saying is don't make it harder on yourself by not doing your best."

"When did you get to be my mama?" he snaps. "I'll be just fine."

I didn't push any further. But I am worried. What's going to happen to us in the fall — Kevin, Li'l Bit, Gabe, J.J., and me?

We are quiet as the day ends in shades of lavender and deep purple. "Just think," says J.J. "We've got the whole summer ahead of us."

CHAPTER FOUR

A Superman Summer

August 1954

This summer has been a Superman Summer — faster than a speeding bullet. Seems no sooner than J.J. said we had the whole summer ahead of us, it's over.

J.J. left right after school for Nashville, Tennessee. Every year he goes to visit his grandparents for the summer. I miss him something awful. But the last week in June, Estelean and I went to the church camp down in the Ozark Mountains. We both came home sun-baked and covered with mosquito bites. We spent the 4th of July at a picnic in Forest Park. Then she went to Mississippi to visit her aunt and cousins.

Mama and I rode the train to Memphis and spent a week visiting with both sets of grandparents. None of my Tennessee cousins are going to integrated schools in September. I guess the Supreme Court hasn't gotten to Tennessee yet.

Come the first week in August, a letter from the school district arrives.

Mama opens the letter and reads it standing in the middle of the living room floor.

"What's it say, Mama?"

"We have an appointment to meet with a Mr. Randolph Keggley on Tuesday, August 10th, at 12:30."

On the day of the appointment, Daddy had to finish repairing one of Seabury Funeral Home's limousines. "If I do this job well, it might mean a big service contract for me," Daddy explains. "You can handle it, Doris." So Mama and I walk to the school together.

Robertson was almost finished. Since spring, I've been watching it change into a large two-story, brick building, encircled by stately pine trees. It looks larger, brighter, and cleaner than any school I've ever seen. As we walk through the two double doors, there are still paint cloths on the floor; ladders and toolboxes are scattered around.

"May I help you?" a woman asks politely.

"My name is Doris Patterson and this is my daughter, Rosemary. We're here for a meeting with Mr. Keggley from Central Office," Mama answers in her very proper, every-subject-and-verb-agreeing-chairman-of-the-committee voice.

"Right this way," says the woman, leading us down a long hall. She introduces herself. "I'm Olivia Lancet, principal of Robertson. Will Rosemary attend here in the fall?"

"Yes," Mama answers.

"Well, welcome, Rosemary," says Mrs. Lancet, smiling at me. "I hope to get to know you better during the school year."

I like the principal instantly. She is very business-like, but there is something soft and loving about her . . . like a grandmother.

But not Mr. Keggley. There is nothing appealing about him.

He is a nervous, little man with quick, bird-like movements. If he wasn't pushing his glasses up on his small nose, he was tapping his fingers on the desk, and add to this a high-pitched voice. What bothers me is that he never looks us in the eye.

"Well, Mrs. ah, ah?" He thumbs through papers, never glancing up. "Mrs. Patterson. Yes. Well, we have your daughter's district placement test scores, and to tell you the truth, they don't look good. The average score is 25. Rosemary's score is 12. Here, see for yourself."

"That is low, but — I don't know what to say. This is so unlike Rosemary." Mama seems uncertain, confused, and that makes me nervous.

Mr. Keggley licks his thumb and begins rifling through another stack of papers. "She's so far below average, we are recommending that Rosemary be transferred to Adams School and placed in a remedial class that we have created for students coming from Attucks."

"No, Mama," I say, pleading. I remember taking that test last spring. It wasn't hard. I just didn't finish it. See, I was sitting by the window and I spied a cloud that looked like the face of Abraham Lincoln. Fascinating. So I started looking for other faces. The bell rang and I had to put my pencil down, even though I wasn't finished with the test.

"Please, Mama, let me explain."

Mama's back stiffens. She hushes me, then turning back to Mr. Keggley, she begins. Her voice steady and sure. "Sir, Rosemary reads and writes beautifully. She wants to be a writer one day. She was the president of her class last year, and she . . ."

Mr. Keggley chuckles and it sounds wicked. "Oh, Mrs. Patterson, none of *that* has anything to do with what we're talking about now."

"But it does," Mama insists. "These numbers don't represent Rosemary's true ability."

Mr. Keggley's face flushes red. He isn't happy with Mama's resistance. "You people need to understand that the expectations will be much higher next year. I'm trying to help the kids from Attucks make a smooth transition."

Still, Mama's position doesn't change. "Attucks has always had top-notch teachers who prepared students to compete in any school environment." Mama's words are like missiles being hurled at Mr. Keggley. "So I don't understand what you mean by, 'the expectations will be much higher next year.' In my mind, they've always been high."

Mr. Keggley shoves his glasses up on his nose and sighs, real disgusted-like. "Okay. Here. I'm going to give Rosemary a little test now to demonstrate what I'm talking about."

Mama gives me a glance. "Don't be nervous, honey."

I try not to be. But my stomach is feathery. This is the kind of thing that might happen to J.J. This can't be happening to *me*.

Mr. Keggley scribbles a big square and puts an opening at the end. "This is a corral," he says. "Do you know what a corral is?"

"Rosemary has never seen a corral . . . how will she . . ." I can hear Mama trying hard to hold onto her proper voice.

"I've read about a corral, though," I assure her. "It's a fenced area where horses are kept."

Mr. Keggley raises an eyebrow in surprise. He makes a stick horse and tells me, "Please draw a line showing how you would get this horse out of the corral."

I take the pencil and think carefully. I want to do this right and prove to Mr. Keggley that I am not remedial. Then an idea comes to me. I will tell a story to get the horse out of the corral. "What's the horse's name?" I ask.

"I'm sorry. . . ." Mr. Keggley sounds surprised and impatient.

"The horse's name," I repeat. "To get the horse out of the corral I need to know his name."

"His name is, uh, uh, Rocky." He waves his hand in disgust.

Mama is looking at me with the same look she gives me when

she's sending me a message without talking. In this case the message is, *Don't do anything stupid.*

I sure didn't intend to.

"Well, first," I begin, "I'll call Rocky, but he won't come, because he sees Blinky, his bird friend, sitting on the tree limb." As part of my story, I draw a line from Rocky to where I imagine Blinky is sitting.

"Then he comes here, to where Quick the Rabbit is eating grass."

I continued to draw the line to the other side of the corral, showing the route Rocky is taking.

"Over here." I continue the line to another corner. "Rocky sees some clover and it tastes so good and sweet." I want to make this special, so I draw a line, bringing the horse to the center of corral.

"Then along comes a butterfly," I say, "and Rocky dances with the butterfly 'round and 'round."

I draw five or six circles in the center of the corral. "Then Rocky finally comes through the gate." I draw a line leading him outside the gate. Then I lay my pencil down.

"Oh," squeals Mr. Keggley, pushing his glasses on his nose again and blinking. "It's worse than I thought." He looks at me as though I was diseased. "Are you beginning to understand now, Mrs. Patterson?"

"What?" asks Mama. "She got the horse out of the corral, just as you asked."

Mr. Keggley hops to his feet. "But what rhyme or reason did she use to do it? You must sign this transfer order."

Mama studies my drawing before speaking again. "Mr. Keggley, you want my daughter to draw a straight line from the horse to the gate. But that's not the way she thinks. Do you have a test for creativity? Mr. Keggley," she says, pulling on her gloves and putting her pocketbook over her arm. Her voice is hardly above a whisper. "You know much more about tests than I do, but I know my daughter is more capable than what those test scores show. And if I have to fight you all the way to the Supreme Court, I'll not allow you to undermine my daughter's confidence. So regrettably, I will not sign any papers." He has only to look in Mama's eyes to know that she means every word.

Taking me by the arm, she leads me out of the room and down the hallway.

"You're only making it hard for your daughter," he says, screeching like an owl.

Mama keeps on walking. I have to run to keep up with her.

As we pass the office, Mrs. Lancet steps out to say good-bye. Instantly, she knows something is wrong. Mama is so visibly shaken. "Mrs. Patterson, what is it? Is there a problem?" Mrs. Lancet asks, insisting that Mama and I come into her office.

Mama explains what Mr. Keggley is recommending. "He wants to put Rosemary in *remedial* classes."

"I'm not dumb," I insist.

"Of course not, dear," Mrs. Lancet answers, smiling. "Being in remedial classes doesn't mean you are mentally deficient. If a student's achievement is behind the district norm, then the student is given help in order to catch up. Nobody is saying you are dumb."

"Yes, ma'am," I answer. Sure. Where I come from, *remedial* means you're dumb and can't learn.

Mama adds quickly, "Remedial is fine if a child needs it. Rosemary doesn't, and I won't sign those transfer papers."

Seeing Mama's resolve, Mrs. Lancet thinks before speaking again. "Okay. Let me speak with Randy — I mean Mr. Keggley. He was a student of mine long ago before I was a principal," Mrs. Lancet says, and excuses herself. She returns in a few minutes with what looks like the same file Mr. Keggley had been reviewing. She studies it.

"Mrs. Patterson, it is true, Rosemary didn't do well on our local placement test. . . ."

"I didn't finish it," I say, jumping in quickly and regretting it when I see Mama's reaction. I shut up immediately.

Mrs. Lancet continues, saying, "Ummm. Here on the state and national tests Rosemary is in the upper percentile. Very impressive. Her classroom grades are consistently good, too."

"I don't understand any of this," Mama says. "Mr. Keggley didn't say a word about Rosemary's other achievement tests."

Mrs. Lancet studies my papers a little more. "Rosemary, you weren't feeling well the day you took the placement test, and that's why you didn't finish? Right?"

"I felt just fi . . ."

"Right," Mama interrupts. "Rosemary sometimes has bad sinus headaches in the morning. Remember, honey?"

"Yes, but . . ."

"Well," says Mrs. Lancet, "that means I have a legitimate reason to use my administrative authority to retest Rosemary. I've been in education long enough to know that when there are conflicting numbers like these, retesting is necessary."

She walks with us to the front door. "Don't worry, I'll retest you at the same time I retest other students who were either ill or absent. We'll get to the bottom of this for sure."

Mama shakes Mrs. Lancet's hand. "You are a fair and caring principal. Rosemary is fortunate to be coming here. Thank you. Thank you."

I agree with Mama. If most of the people are like Mrs. Lancet next year, maybe everything will be okay. But what if there's a school full of Mr. Keggleys? A school full of Draculas couldn't be worse.

On the way home, Mama seems to feel better. "What was all that crazy stuff about the horse in the corral? You know how to draw a straight line, from the horse to the corral gate."

"Sure, Mama," I exclaim, "but I thought by telling a story, Mr. Keggley would see that I'm not remedial. What did I do wrong?"

"You must start thinking like other kids if . . ."

"Okay, Mama," I agree, even though I don't understand.

Mama puts her arm around my waist. We walk along together until she breaks the silence. "Rosemary, there will always be Mr. Keggleys in your life. Don't let him or people who think like him stop you from progressing. Ace that retest like I know you can, baby."

"I'll try."

Mama stops and looks me in the eye. "And forget what I just said. Keep right on thinking like you do. There's more than one way to get a horse out of a corral." There are happy bubbles in Mama's voice, and in the heat of a summer day, her eyes seem to have lights behind them. I'm pleased that I've had something to do with her good mood.

"Let's take the long way home," she says.

I took the retest on the 17th at Kirkland High School. This time I didn't look out the window. Mama got the results a few days ago and a handwritten note from Mrs. Lancet, telling her that I scored in the top percentile of all the students in Kirkland.

"I hope Mr. Keggley puts that in his nose and smells it," I say.

"Watch your mouth," Mama says, adding another seed button

to Frances Pepper's wedding dress. "After all, Mr. Keggley is an adult."

Later, when I'm giving Rags some attention, I hear Mama and Aunt Betty talking about the test.

"I would pay money to have seen Keggley's face when he saw Rosemary's score on the retest," says Aunt Betty.

Mama came back with, "What is it the kids say — I hope he puts that in his nose and smells it!" And she and Aunt Betty fall out laughing. Hard as I try not to laugh, I do.

"Okay in there," Mama calls, but it gets even funnier, because I can hear her choking down a hoot.

Mama's good humor doesn't last very long. Mama and Daddy still snip and snap at each other all the time. Daddy says he can't stand it any longer so he's turned the two rooms over his garage office into a small apartment. He stays there most of the time. Daddy got the big Seabury Funeral Home contract, so he takes care of Mr. Seabury's entire fleet of limousines. Along with his other business, it keeps him pretty busy.

He hardly ever comes home. I miss him, but I don't miss the fighting. Mama misses him. I hear her crying sometimes at night. I wish I can do something to make it all right again — like it was before Miss Jean.

■   ■   ■

Besides my birthday party the greatest part of the summer has been Rags. In spite of all the injuries, she has survived. The horrible wounds have healed, but most of the time she stays in her box. I keep it by the kitchen door in the garage and the first thing I do every morning is greet her. She eats and sleeps, but she doesn't run. She doesn't play. And she doesn't make a sound.

"I love this poor raggedy cat," I say. "She doesn't seem to like me."

"Rags is healing," Mama says, biting a measure of thread. "She's been traumatized. It will take a long while to overcome her physical wounds as well as her emotional ones."

"Do cats have emotions?"

"Of course they do. In time she'll show you how she feels."

School begins the day after Labor Day — less than a week away. I've tried all summer not to think too much about school starting, but now I'm worried.

The one time Mama and Daddy put away their differences is when my schooling is involved. Last week, the board called a meeting with all the colored families with children who live west of Harrison Boulevard. My parents attended. A majority of the colored families who live in Kirkland live east of the boulevard. I hoped it wasn't more about remedial classes and stuff. It wasn't. It's worse.

Mama explains that there are so few colored families with

children scheduled to attend Robertson, the board wants to give those families the option of transferring their children to Adams. "Or you can stay at Robertson," Mama explains. "But you and J.J. will be the only colored kids in the entire sixth grade."

"Even after a month or so, they'll still allow you to change and go to Adams if you wish," Daddy adds. "If you'd rather stay at Robertson, that's okay, too."

I'm thinking about how nice Mrs. Lancet was to me. And I decide to wait and see what happens. "Can I think about it?"

"May I think about it?" Mama corrects me.

"Sure, Mama, you can think about it, too," I tease.

Daddy bursts out laughing. Mama just glares at us both with her soft amber eyes.

It was good to see them together agreeing about something . . . anything.

The official end of summer is September 21, but according to our local calendar, the coming of the Grant-LaSalle Carnival is the harbinger of fall. This year it will occupy the open field at Grant and LaSalle streets, from Wednesday, September 1, to Labor Day, Monday, September 6. The entire county generally shows up for the carnival, but we kids wait for it with the same enthusiasm we wait for Christmas.

I haven't seen much of J.J. since he got back from down south a week ago, because he's been fighting a cold with a fever. Aunt Betty says he's been sleeping a lot, too. But he's looking forward to going with us.

Ordinarily, colored people can attend only one day. The promoters always call it Brotherhood Day. But this year, the carnival is going to be integrated.

From the moment the carnival train rolls into the station, there's excitement in the air. The flyers and posters promise that this year is going to be the best carnival ever — better rides, more sideshows, fun games — but of course, they said all that last year.

J.J. can't wait to see Leo the Lion Man. And I want to be in the front row so I can get a good look at the bearded lady and Jerome the Giant.

For as long as I can remember, Daddy has taken a truckload of us kids from South Kirkland. He even invites the Dead End kids. Some of the older boys come along, but not the Hamiltons. They stand back and glare at us like *we're* the carnival sideshow. The idea of going to school with Grace the Tasteless makes my teeth hurt. I shake the idea out of my head.

Mama isn't coming because she's making a dress for a new client and she wants it to be special. Aunt Betty is staying home with the little ones.

By noon, every kid who's going to the carnival has gathered in front of Daddy's garage. As we're loading up in the back of the truck, I realize J.J. isn't with us. I can't imagine going to Grant-LaSalle without him. But Daddy's about to pull off. "Wait!" I shout. "Let me go see if J.J. is coming. I'll be right back."

"I'm leaving in ten minutes with or without you two," Daddy yells, knowing all the time that he won't leave us — I hope not. That's just his way of saying hurry up.

Hopping off the back of the truck, I take off like a missile. As soon as I turn the corner of Rosebud Street and Harrison, J.J. comes barreling out of his house, head down and legs churning.

"You're gonna get left," I shout, changing directions, heading back to the garage. "Come on!"

"Mama made me eat all the lima beans on my plate," he answers, pretending to gag.

"How many did Aunt Betty make you eat?" I ask, knowing how much J.J. hates lima beans.

"Ten or so."

"That all?"

"One lima bean is too many!" And he pulls a napkin out of his pocket and shakes out eight . . . nine . . . ten lima beans.

At first we jog along side by side. Turning the corner, we see the truck full of our friends. I wave. They wave back and call for us to hurry. Daddy starts the motor and pretends to pull off. Then he stops and yells, "Go, go, go!"

"Beat you to the truck," J.J. says and takes off.

I'm quick to respond and pull ahead of him, but not as easily as I usually do. J.J. is faster and stronger. "You know all promises are off," I say. "Don't say I didn't warn you."

But J.J.'s not giving an inch. He stays close on my back. A few feet from the truck, I feel him beside me . . . and then ahead by a step or two. I pump harder, but my legs won't move me any faster. And J.J. wins by a toe.

I feel light-headed and out of breath as Bevvy pulls me into the back of the truck. It takes a few seconds for the realization to hit me. Even though I am taller and my legs are longer, J.J. has beaten me in a footrace for the first time in our lives . . . and in front of everybody!

Now comes the after talk.

"Man, it looked like Rosemary might do the unthinkable. But we knew you could take her out, and you did it," says Kevin. All the boys pat J.J. on the back.

"I can't help it if I'm good," J.J. says, with his chest stuck out like a fluffed-up rooster. "Hey, I did it and I ain't even been feeling good this week." He coughed to prove his point.

"Baloney!" I say between a huff and a puff of air. I'm all the time imagining J.J. with a shoe stuffed in his mouth . . . my shoe!

"Rosemary, you should know better than to race a boy," says Estelean. "And J.J. especially. You know he's bound to win."

What a nutty idea!

"Rosemary, you are fast *for a girl*," says Gabe.

That's even nuttier.

"Shut up, all of you!" I shout. "So J.J. won a race today. I've beat him many, many times before. Tell them, J.J." I can't believe I'm breaking my promise to him. I try to stop, but I'm too angry. I have to show him up for the fraud that he really is. "Tell them!" I scream.

"Girl, you sound crazy," says Avon, leaning on J.J.'s shoulder. "Charley can't outrun him. I can't outrun him. So how do you figure you can?" Everybody's head is bobbing up and down — even the girls.

"Tell them, J.J.," I keep saying. "Tell them!"

"Tell them what, Rosemary? You're the one talking."

I give J.J. a hard look. He drops his eyes. "You're not my friend anymore, I don't like you, and I may never speak to you again."

The next morning J.J. wakes up with polio.

CHAPTER FIVE

Room 123

September 1954

J.J.'s in the hospital, struggling for his life. As soon as I step inside the door of Robertson Elementary, I want to turn around and run as fast and as far as I can in the opposite direction. First, I can't get over feeling guilty. Mama says it was nothing anybody did. Polio happens to millions of people every year. But I can't help but think that maybe if J.J. hadn't pushed so hard to outrun me he'd be okay now. Or maybe if I hadn't gotten angry with him and said all those hard words. Oh, I know I'm not the cause of J.J.'s polio. But I broke my promise. And that's what's got me feeling so awful . . . and that's not all.

One look around the school and I want to scream. Where do all these white people come from? I'm thinking about what Mama told me. There are two hundred fifty kids in this school — kindergarten through sixth grade — and only fifteen of us are colored.

Even though it's easier getting to school and home — it only takes ten minutes — and there's no busy boulevard to cross or any need to wait for Bevvy, I keep feeling like everything around me is wrong. To start with, the kids have on shorts and pants and tennis shoes, and they're glaring at me as if I've come to a barbecue in a taffeta formal. I'm not exaggerating. I've got on a pink dress with lace on the collar and sleeves, so it may as well be a ball gown. Mama made it special for today, the same as all my first-day outfits at Attucks, except here at Robertson not a single person is dressed up.

It's all wrong!

Perhaps it's because J.J.'s not here with me. I'm thinking, *Why did you have to get sick now, J.J. Stenson?* Then I'm ashamed for fretting about myself when J.J. is in the hospital with polio.

"Probably bought that dress at the Goodwill," I hear two girls whisper. "She looks like one of those dressed-up monkeys they have at the zoo."

They want me to hear their unkind words. A bitter taste rises in my throat. It's not about what they're saying. The Hamiltons have said far worse. But today I am alone. As hard as it is to think about J.J. in the hospital, it is better than being here all by myself.

Add to this, I don't know where to go. And I don't want to ask. I look for Mrs. Lancet.

"May I help you?" a teacher asks. "What's your room number?"

I show her the letter with my teacher's name. "Mrs. Denapolis."

"She's in 123. But first you go to the gym. Okay? That's straight down the hall through the double doors."

"Thank you," I say without thinking.

My mind is totally on J.J. I remember when he refused to give up hope on Rags, even when Daddy had convinced me otherwise. "If she fights, she'll live," I can still hear him saying firmly. I know J.J. is a fighter. So he can lick this polio thing . . . maybe. If only I could be as sure as J.J. was about Rags. But I'm not sure, and that scares me. Thinking about him makes me want to cry. But I force myself to steel up. If J.J. were here he'd say, "Girl, don't give these white kids the opportunity to call you the Chocolate Crybaby." The idea tickles me and I manage a half-smile as I go through the double doors to the gym. Beats crying.

I've never been in a new school before. Everything smells fresh and clean. I'm particularly impressed by the gym's hardwood floor that's so highly polished it looks wet.

Suddenly the microphone squeaks and Mrs. Lancet speaks into it. "Testing . . . testing." All the little kids giggle, even though there isn't a thing that's funny. I feel better seeing her.

"My name is Mrs. Olivia Lancet and I am the principal. Welcome to this wonderfully designed K-6 facility, built just for you, the first students to attend Robertson Elementary." I can't believe Mrs. Lancet gave out her first name. Mr. Richardson, the principal of Attucks, would never tell his.

Jake, the little Beasley boy from up the street, is a kindergartner. Mama keeps him sometimes when Mrs. Beasley has to help at her husband's dry cleaners. Mrs. Lancet welcomes the fidgety kindergartners. I'm thinking little Jake will never know about going to an all-black school. Whatever happens in my future, I don't ever want to forget my Attucks years.

Next, Mrs. Lancet gives instructions about the rest of the day. Then she concludes with: "I just know the 1954–55 school year is going to be the best year ever for all of us." Principals must be taught to speak the same way — no matter what their race.

We are dismissed to go to our classes. As the kids file out, I'm thinking how much I'm going to miss Attucks . . . Estelean . . . and all the rest.

Now I'm trying to find Mrs. Denapolis in room 123. I figure it's on the first floor, so I follow the numbers in rising order. Kids along the way make me feel like I've got antlers growing out the sides of my head or that something else weird is going on. At last I find room 123. I stand outside the door taking long, deep breaths. Then I open the door and whose ugly face do I see first thing? Grace the Tasteless Hamilton.

Grace takes one look at my dress and bellows, "What kind of getup is that?"

My first thought is to run again — run as fast and as far away as my legs will take me. I don't want to go to school here and I'm never coming back — even if it means I must go to remedial school.

"Come in," says a young woman rushing over to greet me. "You look lovely."

Baloney!

But she's so pleasant, she almost seems believable. "I'm Mrs. Helen Denapolis, your teacher." I like that she's not syrupy or gushy nice. But best of all she has a smile that sits comfortably on her lips. She makes me want to smile back.

"Come join us. We're just getting started with our seating chart." Mrs. Denapolis has us line up along the wall while she assigns us seats. I keep my eyes glued to the floor. I'm in the fifth row, seat one. And as my luck would have it, Grace Hamilton is in the fourth row, seat one — next to me.

I wonder where the rest of the class is, but then I realize there are only going to be twenty-five of us. Mama was real happy when she heard that. I've never been in a class this small, but I don't know a single person in the room — except that awful Grace Hamilton.

I never thought coming to school would be this bad. I tell myself that I will transfer to Adams as soon as I can.

But in the meantime, I've got to get another seat assignment. I'd rather sit on the roof than sit next to Grace the Tasteless. As the other kids are putting things in their newly assigned desks, Grace and I almost knock each other over trying to get to Mrs. Denapolis's desk. "I would like permission to move away from *her*," I say before Grace gets a chance to speak.

"Yes, I'd like to move, too." Grace nudges me. I shove her back.

"Wait a minute here," says Mrs. Denapolis. "What is going on between you two? Do you even know each other?"

"Yes, I know her," I say, glaring at Grace the Tasteless. "She's always picking on me. Like now. She shoved me first."

"Not so. Was her," Grace argues.

"Please? Will you move my seat?" I beg.

Mrs. Denapolis thinks for a moment. "Let's leave things the way they are for now. I'll give your requests some thought and make a decision later."

So much for Mrs. Denapolis being nice.

Grace sits with her back to me, arms folded, her bottom lip poked out, pouting like a kindergartner. I turn in the opposite direction, so I don't have to look at the back of her head.

I heard Mrs. Denapolis call the boy to my right Stuart Weissman. His foot is in a cast. "I broke it horseback riding at our ranch in Arizona," he says, trying to smile.

"Horseback riding? Ranch? Arizona? Is your father some kind of millionaire?" I ask.

"Well . . . yes," Stuart answers matter-of-factly.

I laugh. Then I realize Stuart isn't joking.

The girl sitting behind me is wearing inch-thick glasses, and the boy behind Grace has on a hearing aid. It's like a riddle. *What's cripple, and almost blind, and hard of hearing and stupid?* All of us special kids sitting together. Mrs. Denapolis must think I need help because I'm the only colored kid in class.

"I am originally from Providence, Rhode Island," Mrs. Denapolis tells us. "But I graduated from the University of Missouri. My husband and I live here because he is an intern in pediatrics at Barnes Hospital."

I'm trying to listen, but suddenly I realize that the empty desk behind Stuart is where J.J. was supposed to sit. Hard as I try, I can't stop the tears. I cover my face with my hands.

Mrs. Denapolis takes me to the bathroom.

"Don't be frightened," she says as she hands me a paper towel to wash my face. "I know the first day is always hard, but it will get better."

Oh, she's thinking that I'm crying because I am the only colored girl in class. I feel like the biggest loser of all time. In this corner, the Chocolate Crybaby.

"I'm fine now," I say.

"Sure?"

"Very sure!" I'll say anything to get out of here. This is the most terrible beginning of school I've ever had.

School lets out at 12:30 — not a moment too soon. I kick off my shoes and dash home. I'm anxious to tell Mama I want to transfer and to hear how J.J. is doing. But first, I stop off at Mr. Bob's to buy myself a treat. I deserve one.

"There's a storm brewing in your face," he says. "Was the first day that bad?"

"Mr. Bob, it was awful. Way, way awful."

"A lot of name-calling?"

"Some. But it could have been worse. The hardest part was not having any of my friends there with me, especially J.J."

"The wife and I heard about J.J. and we're sick at heart. The whole community is praying for him," says Mr. Bob. "Hang in there," Mr. Bob adds. "You are a pioneer in the real sense of the word, Rosemary. Whenever you are the first, you're going to have it hard. I was in the Army–Air Force during World War II. They said colored men couldn't fly airplanes, especially in combat. But we Tuskegee pilots proved ourselves repeatedly. So, I say this to you so you'll maybe gather strength from my words. Be the best you can be, and that's all anybody can ask."

"Thank you, Mr. Bob," I say, and hurry home.

Mama and Daddy are sitting at the kitchen table, talking. It's strange, seeing Daddy home during the day. In fact, Daddy stayed over last night, so Mama could sit with Aunt Betty. Mama's eyes are rimmed in red. "Is . . . is J.J. dead?" I ask.

"No, no, dear," Mama answers quickly. "J.J. is still in critical condition, but he's stabilizing. He will live. . . ."

"Then he's okay, huh?" I ask. "When will he be able to come home? Go to school?"

Mama gives Daddy a look that tells me they know something they don't want me to know.

Mama changes the subject from J.J. to school. "Tell us, Rosemary.

What was it like?" she asks, trying to sound cheery. "Is your teacher nice? Did you make any new friends? Tell us everything."

"It's a pretty school, but it's full of white kids and all white teachers."

Daddy shakes his head, but he doesn't say anything. I didn't tell them that at Robertson they don't dress up on first day, like we did at our school. And I don't tell them about the mean things kids said to me. I want to say something about the transfer right then, but instead I talk about how the gym floor was very shiny.

"Yes, but tell us about your teacher and how the kids received you."

When I think about how much J.J. is going through, I decide not to complain about a few bad stares and nasty words.

"Mrs. Denapolis is as nice as Mrs. Lancet," I tell Mama. "But she sat me next to that horrible Dead End girl, Grace Hamilton. I wished for J.J. a hundred times," I say, but I'm all the time thinking, *If I had known he wasn't going to be with me, I would have never agreed to go to Robertson Elementary . . . and be by myself in that class.*

Suddenly, I am trembling with emotion. Mama hugs me close. "We all knew it wasn't going to be easy, Rosemary. But if it's too bad, we can always make changes."

I shake my head. "It's not about school," I say.

"Rosemary, there is something you need to know," Daddy begins.

"Please don't," Mama puts in, but Daddy interrupts. "We

can't shield bad things from Rosemary forever. J.J. is her friend. She needs to know the truth and be prepared for it." Turning to me, he continues. "Listen, honey, polio is not like a cold that J.J. can just get over. He could have died. Some people do. Fortunately he will live, but he's paralyzed from his waist down."

"Will he walk or run ever again?" I ask, wiping tears from my stinging eyes.

"Probably not," says Mama. "But he's alive. J.J. is alive. Be grateful for that."

"Grateful? I'm grateful for a birthday gift, food, a new dress," I shout. "But I'm not grateful for my friend being paralyzed instead of dead." I run to my room and allow myself to cry and cry and cry — about J.J., school, Mama, Daddy. All of it.

Later, sitting on the back steps, listening to the radio, I lift Rags from her box and place the little cat in my lap. "You surprised us all," I say. "J.J. is strong. He's going to surprise a lot of people when he walks — no, when he runs again."

Rags stares up at me with one good eye. "I kept my promise to J.J. all year. I never outran him in front of his buddies. Then he won in a fair race and I couldn't take it. But I'm so sorry." Rags is such a good listener. "I'm ready to make a new promise and you are my witness," I say. "I will never stop believing that J.J. will run again. Cross my heart and hope to die." Rags blinks and licks her paws.

■　　■　　■

At church on Sunday, I get to visit with my old classmates — Gabe, Kevin, and, of course, Estelean. All the talk's about J.J. In a strange way, he would love all this attention, but never at the cost of not walking. Even J.J. wouldn't go to that extreme.

Prayers are offered up for the Stenson family and J.J.'s name has been put on the sick-and-shut-in list. That seems so strange to me. Mostly old folks are on the sick-and-shut-in list, not a ten-year-old boy.

The four of us sit together in the last pew in the back of the church balcony so we can talk softly.

"J.J.'s got polio," says Gabe. "Man-oh-man that's bad!"

I nod. "But he'll be all right."

"Somebody tol' us he was paralyzed from the neck down, and he's being kept alive by an iron lung," Kevin says.

"That ain't so," I reply, a little too loud, drawing stares from the mothers in the front pew. "He's just paralyzed from his waist down."

"But didn't you just say he was going to be all right?" Estelean puts in.

"He is," I insist.

"Being paralyzed and unable to walk ain't all right," Kevin argues.

"But I believe that he's going to walk again," I say.

They're silent, because they don't know what to say. Or they're afraid of saying the wrong thing. To them, J.J. is one of the unlucky ones who has polio. They're glad "it" didn't get them. Yet, they feel guilty that it didn't. Me included.

To get us all off the hook, I change the subject. "What's it like at Adams?" I ask.

"A lot of white folks. Even the janitors and the cooks are white," says Kevin.

"All wrong," I say, nodding my head.

"I didn't even know white folks cooked and cleaned," said Gabe. "I thought those jobs were reserved for colored people."

We all lean over like we're tying our shoes so Reverend Cole won't know we're laughing.

"What's it like at Robertson?" Kevin asks me.

"Well, the principal is nice. I met her this summer. And my teacher seems to be okay. But guess who's in my class and sits right next to me?"

"Who?"

"Grace Hamilton!"

"Yuck! I'd rather sit by a martian than her," says Estelean. The two of them have had more than a few run-ins, too.

"Her brother, Marty Hamilton, is at Adams," Gabe puts in. "He's such a troublemaker."

Kevin adds, "He's in the remedial classes with a lot of colored kids. He's already been in two fights."

"Are there a lot of colored kids in remedial?" I ask, remembering Mr. Keggley.

"A lot! But not one person from Mrs. Washington's class is in remedial. But Jubal Luckett is doing sixth grade again, and so is Theronia Michaels."

I'm thinking how glad I am Mama stood her ground with Mr. Keggley.

"Our teacher this year at Adams is Mrs. Foxworthy," Estelean whispers, "and she looks like a little pointed-nosed *fox* who ain't *worthy* of nothing."

I cover my mouth to catch a giggle, but it escapes and fills the sanctuary. I feel Mama giving me the *look* from the choir loft. I may be in trouble, but it's been worth it to share a few moments with my friends.

It's been several weeks since school started and I've settled into a routine in room 123. I really like Mrs. Denapolis, more than I thought possible. She sure sounds better than Mrs. Foxworthy. Most of the kids in 123 leave me alone. I eat by myself and go out on the playground at recess and read.

The real eye-opener has been watching Grace the Tasteless at school, especially around Katherine Hogan. Now that girl's something out of the Wizard of Odd. Talk about being awful, terrible, and mean. But Katherine's not all bad. She hates Grace! The truth is, white kids don't like Grace anymore than I do. In fact, they treat her the same way they treat me.

I was shocked to see Grace eating by herself too. At recess, she stands by and looks on, but the other girls never invite her to jump rope or hopscotch. When she's at home with her family, she seems larger, meaner, and tougher. With her brother Snot-nosed Marty at Adams this year, that puts Grace here at Robertson alone — a lot like me without J.J. So, it's hard for her to show her toughness.

Katherine Hogan, a redhead with green eyes and freckles, has most of the girls in class eating out of her hand. When I look at that girl, all I see is one huge mouth with all kinds of garbage tumbling out of it. I've started calling her Katherine the Great Mouth.

Grace would love nothing more than for Katherine to include her in their jack games and card swaps. But unless Katherine gives the okay, the other girls won't come near Grace.

On the playground, I'm sitting on a bench trying to read. "Arkansas trash, and a porch monkey," a couple of fifth-grade girls whisper to each other, just loud enough for Grace to hear and me, too. "What next?"

When Grace realizes that I've heard the comment, she turns on me. "What are you looking at, monkey-girl?" she scowls. The fifth graders laugh and move on.

"Excuse me, Miss Arkansas Trash," I say ever so politely. "Did you say something to me?" That shuts her up with a quickness. But it doesn't make me feel good.

■　　■　　■

After noon recess, when I get back to class, Katherine the Great Mouth is weeping and wailing, her body convulsing in shoulder-shaking sobs. Mrs. Denapolis is trying to console her.

Blind Bart can see she's as full of stuff as a Thanksgiving turkey.

It tickles me. Until out of nowhere, she points in my direction and shouts, "She stole it! I know she did."

"What?" I ask.

"My sweater, that's what," she hisses. All the tears dry up instantly. I can't believe she's accusing me of stealing. And for what reason?

"You're always losing your sweater," Grant, one of the boys, puts in. Laughter spreads throughout the room.

Nothing's funny about this situation. I don't have her sweater and that should be it. But no, Katherine is not to be denied.

Mr. Denapolis frowns. "Calm down, all of you."

But there is no calming down. Katherine screams at the top of her lungs. "I know that girl has my sweater!"

"How do you know?" Mrs. Denapolis asks.

Katherine rushes over to Grace. "You saw Rosemary take my sweater, didn't you? Didn't you, Grace? You know how *they* steal."

Grace is surprised that she's been brought into this. Looking around wildly, she figures it's a chance to make me pay for all the fights we've had. She nods. "Yes, I seen Rosemary —"

"You saw her what?" asks Mrs. Denapolis. I can hear anger in Mrs. Denapolis's voice. I'm all the time hoping she's not believing a word of this lie.

Grace swallows hard. "Yes. I *saw* her take Katherine's sweater," Grace whispers. Liar! It is written all over her face. Then it hits me. This isn't about me. This is about Grace wanting to be accepted by Katherine so badly, she's willing to lie to get her approval. I am too upset to answer.

Mrs. Denapolis faces us. "Rosemary, you've been accused by two people," she says, trying to stay in control. She bites her bottom lip, a habit she has when she's nervous. "Did you take the sweater, Rosemary?"

"No," I answer, directly. Then, forcing myself to hold my head up, I add, "I have four or five sweaters of my own. I don't need to steal another one." I open my satchel and desk for all to see. No sweater.

Mrs. Denapolis nods. "Katherine, Grace, now what do you have to say for yourselves? You have accused a person of stealing, but where is your evidence?

"I still think *she* has it," says Katherine. "She's probably hidden it somewhere."

"That's enough," says Mrs. Denapolis. "We will . . ."

Suddenly, a hall monitor appears at the door. "We found this sweater in the hallway. Does it belong to anyone here?"

"Told you," says Billy. "Katherine's always losing stuff and blaming other people."

Katherine doesn't want to claim her own sweater, but everybody knows it's hers. She snatches it from the student and goes to her seat with that smart-aleck smirk on her face.

Mrs. Denapolis insists that Katherine and Grace apologize to me.

"I'm so, so sorry," says Katherine in a fake sweet voice.

"Sorry," Grace mumbles.

I don't know why teachers make kids say stuff they don't mean. Their apologies are meaningless. And so is my acceptance.

I don't mention a word about the sweater incident to Mama. I figure it will only upset her more and she's got plenty to be worried about. Daddy comes home less and less. We haven't seen Daddy all week. I go by the shop, but he's never there. Mr. Logan promises to give him my messages, but Daddy hasn't come by the house or called.

"Has Daddy stopped loving us, Mama?" I ask.

"Never think that your father doesn't love you. He's confused right now. But no matter what happens between the two of us, he loves you dearly."

I used to believe that he did, but I'm not convinced that it's true anymore.

J.J.'s condition isn't any worse, but it's no better, either, so that's got Mama in a tangle of worry, too. She's been helping Aunt Betty night and day, doing anything she can. Plus Mama's got her sewing business, and sewing for people can be a nightmare. "Doris, this isn't right." "Doris change this." "Change that!" I don't want to add any more to her worries.

So, I tell Rags my problems. She's the perfect listener. Never gives me a word back.

At school the next morning, Mrs. Denapolis closes the door as she steps inside to begin the day. First, we stand and sing the Star-Spangled Banner, and repeat the Pledge of Allegiance. We have to remember to say the phrase "under God" that's been added to the pledge this year. Most of the things we do here at Robertson are the same as those we did at Attucks.

We recite the Lord's Prayer or the 23rd Psalm. Then afterward, we listen to the announcements and lunch menu — meatballs and spaghetti today. Everybody cheers, same as we did at Attucks.

Mrs. Denapolis writes the word for the day on the chalkboard: *tolerance*. And as usual, Mrs. Denapolis asks one of us to look up the word and use it in a sentence.

"Grace, will you do us the honor?" says Mrs. Denapolis.

After a moment to find it in the dictionary, Grace reads, "Tolerance is a fair and objective attitude toward opinions and practices that are different from one's own."

From that point on, the day was no longer "as usual."

"I want all the blue- and green-eyed people to come up front," says Mrs. Denapolis. When they have gathered around the blackboard, she lets the bomb drop. "You aren't going to be able to go to the lunchroom today. You will have to eat here in this room, by yourselves, away from the others."

"Why?" asks Billy.

"Because somebody told me that blue-eyed people are thieves and green-eyed people are liars, so I don't want those kinds of students around my other students."

Is she serious? She sure looks like it. But Mrs. Denapolis is way too nice to be that cruel. So there's got to be a reason.

"It's not fair," Katherine puts in. Naturally she would say that, because she's green-eyed.

"Oh. I've always been told green-eyed people are inferior," says Mrs. Denapolis. "Not too smart, a little bit slow . . . if you know what I mean," and she chuckles wickedly. Mrs. Denapolis is really pouring it on.

After lunch, some of the kids are almost in tears.

"So what has this been about?" asks Mrs. Denapolis.

Stuart raises his hand. "I know," he says. "You've been saying unfair stuff about blue- and green-eyed people, the way colored people are sometimes judged."

Mrs. Denapolis smiles. "Right, but not just colored people. Anybody who is not the same."

"Like Jews," says Stuart.

"And Chinese," said Jason Lee, the only Asian boy in our class.

Then one by one, the students begin to understand.

"How did you feel when I said you were a thief simply because you had blue eyes," she asks, "or that you weren't smart just because of your eye color? Billy?"

"I didn't like it," he answers. "It isn't fair."

Grace is sitting at her desk, arms folded, head down.

"We are all prejudiced about something," Mrs. Denapolis explains. "I don't like winter. No reason. I just don't like cold weather. I am prejudiced about winter. But winter isn't wrong and neither are the people who enjoy snow."

Mrs. Denapolis goes on to say that her grandfather was from Greece. "He came to this country in 1908. Some people were prejudiced against immigrants. They made fun of his accent and what he ate and the way he worshipped. My father was born in America and so was I, so we don't have the same problems as Grandpa did. But I grew up listening to his stories."

She wrote the word on the blackboard in all capital letters. TOLERANCE. "This is our class word for the whole year. We're going to learn the deeper meaning of this word day by day."

We know she is finished when she says, "Turn to page 23 in your math books."

I'm all the time thinking I can't wait to tell Mama about what happened today.

CHAPTER SIX

Putting Tolerance to the Test

October 1954

After social studies, Mrs. Denapolis takes a moment to tell the class about J.J.

"As you know, James Johnson Stenson was supposed to be in this class, but on Labor Day he was diagnosed with polio. He hasn't officially been removed from my roll book, so technically he's still a member of this class. And I think we should write him letters, introducing ourselves and wishing him well."

"What do you write to a stranger?" Katherine whines.

"Whatever you wish," Mrs. Denapolis answers.

It is so quiet in the class you could hear an ant crawling on cotton.

Turning to me, Mrs. Denapolis says, "Rosemary, J.J. was your classmate last year. Tell us something about him."

I didn't want to stand up and talk in front of the class. No way.

Then I see a smirk on Grace's face, and Katherine looks bored. "Okay, Mrs. Denapolis." I jump right in, talking fast, the way I do when I'm nervous. "I have known J.J. Stenson since we were in kindergarten. We live next door to each other and until this year, we walked to school together every day."

Talking relaxes me a little and I slow down. "J.J. runs like the wind, but he could never outrun me — except the day before he was stricken with polio. Now he's paralyzed. They say he'll never walk again. But I know better. He's going to walk again! I know he will." I sit down.

Nobody says anything.

"Thank you, Rosemary," says Mrs. Denapolis.

And the class spends the afternoon writing letters.

The next day at recess, three boys are waiting for me at the bottom of the steps: Howie, Billy, and Stuart, who is still on crutches. I call them the Three Blind Mice, because they follow behind one another like little mice. I brace for the trouble I feel is coming.

"Are you really that fast?" Stuart asks. "Fast enough to beat a boy?"

"Yeah," I say. "Faster than any one of you." I've seen them run, so I'm confident.

"I don't believe you," says Billy.

"You're gonna have to prove it," says Howie.

I've been challenged. And the challenge is accepted. We head for the playground. The girls quickly pass the word and room 123 gathers for the race. Howie and Billy are on either side of me.

On your mark. Get set. Go!

For a split second I'm thinking maybe I should pull back, let one of them beat me. No way. I hear Mama telling me never to hold back. I pick up speed. In a few seconds, it's over. A piece of cake. I win without even trying hard.

"You're good," says Howie, flashing a woodchuck smile.

"How'd you learn to run so fast?" asks Billy.

Stuart hobbles away, but he calls over his shoulder. "If J.J. beat *you*, he must have been a bullet."

"He didn't beat me but once," I shout back. ". . . and I had on my good shoes!"

The boys are gone. No one is left but the girls. Katherine doesn't know what to say — yet. I head for my favorite bench where I sit and read everyday. A light glint catches my eye. I look up. Mrs. Denapolis is standing at the window with a huge grin on her face.

Rags still clings to her box. She won't meow, or purr, or make any sound. She loves me to rub her stomach and tickle her paws, so I do it often to keep her happy. I wish human happiness was as easy to achieve.

I feel so sorry for Aunt Betty and Uncle John. Their whole life seems to be turned inside out. Aunt Betty stays at the hospital with J.J. all day, every day. Uncle John has to work, so somebody has to take care of the house and look after Josh and Bootsie. So

Aunt Betty's sister has come to help out, but she can't stay but a few more days.

Meanwhile, Mama told me yesterday that J.J. got the letters the class wrote earlier in the week. "He enjoyed reading them so much, especially yours."

"Do you think he would like for me to write him again?" I ask, hoping he's forgiven me for being such a poor sport.

"Girl, you know he'd rather hear from you than anybody!" Aunt Betty says. If writing a letter can help J.J., then I'll write one every week, every day. Now!

Right away I begin writing J.J. how I won a race against two of the boys in class.

Hurry and get better so we can beat them together.

Your friend,

Rosemary

I enjoy Saturdays because I get to spend time with Estelean. She comes by early and we head for the city park. Along the way, she gives me all the news from Adams.

"You know how Avon James is always doing stuff," she explains.

"I sure do. Remember when he called Mrs. Washington by her first name?" We laugh.

"Uh-hum," Estelean goes on. "Kevin, Gabe, and I bet Avon that he couldn't balance five geography books on his head and walk from the back of the room to the front. He took the bet. But halfway up the aisle, Mrs. Foxy-Loxy — that's what we call her — walked in. Avon lost his balance and books fell all over the place. She sent Avon to the office, talkin' 'bout how he abused school property."

"Just for that?"

"Girl, his mama had to take off from work and come to the school to clear it up," Estelean puts in.

The more I hear my friends talk, the more I realize I'm glad I didn't transfer to Adams.

"You'd better be glad you didn't get sent to Adams," she assures me, talking so fast I can hardly understand her. "Our teacher is so prejudiced." Estelean's eyes look twice their size behind her glasses. "Nothing we do is right." She's twitching and moving like a frightened little bird. "You know how smart Marian Ambry is?"

"Sure."

"Well, the highest grade she's about to get out of Foxy-Loxy is a B. Marian hasn't gotten a B in her life."

I remember Mr. Keggley and how he made me feel like I was stupid.

All I can think to say is what Mr. Bob told me. "Hold on. Don't give up. We are pioneers, the first group to integrate, so we're going to have to put up with more than the next group behind us."

"I hope you're right," she says. "I'm holding on, but . . ."

On my way home from the park, I stop at Mr. Bob's Grocery Store to buy a PayDay. All at once, Snot-nosed Marty and Grace the Tasteless come in. They look around as if casing the joint for a heist. *Heist.* That's a word I've been wanting to use, since I heard it on *Gang Busters.* Anyway, Marty stands near the magazines and potato chips up front. Grace goes to the back where the meat counter is located. Mr. Bob calls out, "May I help you with something?"

"I'd like to buy 10 cents' worth of pickle-loaf lunchmeat," Grace says. Mr. Bob doesn't seem to notice how nervous she's acting. I do. Meanwhile, I duck behind the bread where I can see Marty, but he can't see me. Marty grabs two bags of potato chips and slips out the door.

I've never witnessed a burglary — a real heist — before. I remember back at Attucks when Jackie Fuller found a dime on the floor between his desk and Margaret Bookers. Margaret insisted that the dime had fallen out of her pocket. Jackie claimed it was his, saying, "Finders keepers, losers weepers." We all knew the dime belonged to Margaret. So in my mind, Jackie was *almost* a thief. "Marty Hamilton is a criminal — just like Jesse James," I whisper to myself.

I wonder if I should tell. But I don't want to be a tattler . . . not even on the Hamiltons, but I feel something should be said.

About that time, Mr. Bob comes up front with Grace. She's as white as a sheet, and her hands are shaking. Guilty. She speaks softly. "Hi, Rosemary."

She never speaks to me, especially after lying about me stealing Katherine's sweater. When all the time, she's the liar and the thief.

"How's J.J.?" she asks.

"What do you care?"

"Rosemary . . ." Mr. Bob doesn't have to say any more. As my Sunday school teacher, he expects me to be kind, even to a Hamilton. I wonder if he would feel that way if he knew her brother had just clipped him for two bags of chips.

"J.J.'s still in the hospital. They are working on his legs," I say, speaking more to Mr. Bob than to Grace.

Grace doesn't say any more. She puts a dime on the counter to pay for the small package of lunchmeat. There's not a mean bone in Mr. Bob's body. But he raises an eyebrow and says in a voice that would scare the ugly off a monster, "Thank you, Grace. But how would you like me to take care of the two bags of potato chips Marty took? Should I add the cost to your mother's account?"

Grace is frozen in terror. Her face is milk white, and her mouth drops open. Then she begins turning red . . . and redder . . . and redder. "Yes, sir, add it to Mama's account," she whispers and hurries away. The door clanks shut behind her with a thud.

"Error punishes itself," says Mr. Bob. "Grace is embarrassed, as well she should be." He clicks his teeth. "The Hamiltons aren't bad kids. They're just confused."

"Why didn't you call the police?" I ask.

"Why didn't you tell me that Marty had stolen chips?"

I can't answer.

"Actually, this is the first time I've caught them red-handed."

Mr. Bob points to a mirror on the meat counter that reflects a clear view of the front. "I'm surprised that Grace was involved. She's the nicest one of the bunch."

Baloney!

That's like saying a cobra is not as dangerous as other snakes. "What more can you expect from the Hamiltons," I put in, paying for the cat food.

"Don't be guilty of the same wrong that has been done to you." Mr. Bob goes on, almost talking to himself. "I know Mrs. Hamilton is trying her best, so when she comes in, I will speak to her about what happened. No need to involve the police right now."

Mr. Bob leans on his elbows and looks at me squarely in the face. "But listen to me, little lady. Don't allow anybody to steal your decency. Let your words and deeds be kind and generous, for your own sake."

"What if people are mean to you first? Do you still keep treating them kind and generous?"

"Yes, especially then."

"You sound like my teacher, Mrs. Denapolis," I say. "She says we need to practice tolerance."

"Listen to your teacher. She sounds like a wise lady," he says with a nod and a wink. "By the way, how's that little cat you rescued?"

"The same . . ." Then I quickly add, "But she's going to get better."

■   ■   ■

The next day, the dismissal bell rings, and I'm out of the door and halfway home when I hear someone calling my name. Looking back, I see Grace the Tasteless, half skipping, half hopping to catch up with me.

"What do you want?" I ask impatiently.

"I just wanted to say . . . to say . . . to say, I'm sorry."

"Okay, what? What do you want? What is it?"

"Look, I'm not trying to pick a fight or nothing. . . ."

"You've already picked a fight when you lied to impress Katherine, hoping she might like you. She doesn't, you know. And she never will. She hates you about as much as you hate me." My harsh words make Grace look away.

I'm deliberately being harsh. Mr. Bob would be so disappointed in me, but Mr. Bob doesn't have to put up with Grace all day. "Nobody likes a liar — and a thief, too," I add. "I can't believe you stole from Mr. Bob. Shucks, girl, you're a strikeout any way you hit it."

Grace looks angry now, but she doesn't act like I expect her to. "I did lie on you, and I'm sorry for that. I hardly ever lie." She sounds like it's important for me to know that about her. "And I don't steal. I didn't have anything to do with . . ." She swallows. It is hard for her to go on. "Mr. Bob, he's always been decent to Ma and me. But now he thinks I stole from him, because you tattled on us."

Now I'm shocked. "I did no such thing," I say defensively. "He's got mirrors all around his store. He saw you with his own eyes."

Grace stops walking, "Mirrors? I — I thought you told to get back at me about the sweater thing. Well, anyway, for your information I'm not a thief. I knew my brother was going to steal those chips. I warned him not to do it, but he did anyway. When I told Pops, Marty got a beatin'."

"He should have . . ."

I'm thinking then about what Mr. Bob said about Grace being the best of the lot. Maybe she isn't a thief. But she's still mean.

"Marty ate both bags of chips," she says, sounding real put out, "and didn't offer me one!"

For some strange reason, that strikes me as funny. The idea of *me* laughing with a *Hamilton* is a joke all by itself.

"So I was wrong about you telling on me," she says.

"And I was wrong for thinking you were in on the chip-stealing." Then I add quickly, "But you still lied on me. Now you know how it feels to be accused of something you didn't do."

Grace nods. "I'm sorry." I feel this time she really means it.

"I accept your apologies," I say.

Grace turns toward Dead End and I head home. "Hey," she calls. "If you tell *anybody* my brother's a thief, I'll never speak to you again."

Now that's the Grace the Tasteless I know.

"You never speak to me anyway," I yell back. "Try something else, like you'll send one of your spooky brothers to grind up my bones or something. That might work."

"Rosemary Patterson, you're a weirdo."

"Look who's talking."

Fall in Kirkland looks like a giant went berserk and threw paint in every direction. I sit on the back porch and write in my journal. Splashes of orange, red, and yellow dazzle the eyes in the mid-October sun. Late-blooming flowers dance the last dance with the wind.

On one of those beautiful afternoons, I come in and find Aunt Betty having coffee with Mama at the kitchen table.

"I sure hope Mel gets some sense and comes back home," she says. But seeing me, she quickly changes the conversation.

"We have wonderful news about J.J., dear," Mama says, managing a fake smile. I know because her eyes are far too dark.

Aunt Betty takes over from there. "J.J.'s doctor," she explains, "told me about a program at Meharry Hospital in Nashville, Tennessee, where they treat polio victims with hydrotherapy."

"Hydrotherapy? How does it work?" I ask, hoping it isn't something scary and painful.

"Physical therapists put patients in a tub of hot — very hot — churning water. This helps stimulate the muscles. Some patients — with the help of braces — have been able to regain movement. And walk." Aunt Betty seems so excited.

She rushes on with her explanation. "What really lifted J.J.'s spirits is what the doctor told him about a girl from Clarksville, Tennessee, who had a severe case of polio. But after hydrotherapy, she's now able to play high school basketball and run track, as well. The doctor says we should remember this girl's name, because we're going to hear about her again and again. She's some kind of sprinter. Wilma Rudolph."

"Faster than me?" I ask.

"Oh, no, not the speeding bullet," Aunt Betty teases. Then she gets serious again. "These treatments are going to take time . . . years maybe, and a lot of money. But John and I are committed to getting the best care for J.J. that we can."

Mama pats Aunt Betty's hand. "It's gonna be alright."

"Yes, and it's going to be fine with you, too," she tells Mama.

I can't wait to open J.J.'s letter. As usual, he's short and to the point. Still, it's so good seeing his handwriting, the special way he dresses up his capital letters with swirls and curls.

Dear Rosemary,

I got the class letters. Got your separate letter, too. I'm going to Nashville to be treated at Meharry Hospital. I'll see you one day soon, I hope. I accept your apologies for getting mad at me for running past you, like a super 8. I like hearing about how you left those white boys in the wind. I also liked hearing about our cat, Rags. Take good care of her until I get home and can outrun you again!

Your friend,
J.J.

I guess I won't be seeing J.J. in a long, long while, since he's transferring to Meharry right away. Aunt Betty's sister and Mama are busy helping Aunt Betty pack up Bootsie and Josh for the long drive to Nashville. Uncle John looks so sad, seeing his family preparing to leave. He has to stay here for his job and to take care of the house.

One look at Mama's eyes and I realize that she's very sad, too, because her best friend is moving away. I remind myself to do something to lighten her eyes.

October is my favorite month, because it's beautiful, but also because it's Halloween. It's on Sunday this year, but we're going to celebrate at school on Friday.

Mrs. Denapolis says we're going to invite Mrs. Noble's first-grade class to our party, and they'll be the judges in the best costume contest.

We all groan. "What do little kids know about judging our costumes?" Stuart asks.

"Come on now," says Mrs. Denapolis. "It will be fun."

Katherine is letting everybody know that her annual Halloween party is going to be on October 30. "At the Windover Country Club," she says, as though describing a delicious dessert.

Every girl in class would cut off a toe to get an invitation to that party. But nobody wants to be invited more than Grace. And Katherine knows it. That's why she hasn't been invited. Why doesn't Grace get it? Blind Boone could see through Katherine on a cloudy day.

During recess, Katherine comes over to me, real friendly-like. I know she's up to something, but I can't figure out what. Then she hits me with it. "Rosemary, if you want to be included then you have to start being more, well, like us."

"Is that right?" I say, sounding interested enough for her to go on.

"If you let me, I can fix it where you'll be in the group. All you need is a word from me and the girls will fall into line. What do you say?"

"Well, I don't know," I say, sounding like I still might be convinced.

"I'll even invite you to my party," she says, smiling sweetly. Then she tells me the clincher. "You will have to do one thing to convince us that you're one of us."

"What is that?" I ask, equally as pleasing.

"We all hate Grace. She's such a jellyfish. We're going to catch her in the bathroom and all of us are going to call her poor white trash. It'll really get her if *you* are with us. Say you will and all your troubles are over."

What?

My expression should have been an answer enough. But to make sure she understood me, I say, "Look. I've called Grace poor white trash so many times it would be meaningless coming from me anyway. But I wouldn't call her anything just to be friends with *you*. So get out of my face."

Katherine leans over to whisper in my ear. "You're going to be sorry."

A day or so later, I'm in the bathroom washing my hands. Grace comes out of a stall. Suddenly Katherine and a couple of her flunkies corner Grace. I'm trying not to pay them any attention, but I can't help but overhear.

"I have one last invitation to my party," Katherine the Great Mouth says. "All you have to do is . . ." and she whispers something in Grace's ear.

I bolster my courage, because I know what's coming. Quickly drying my hands, I hurry to get out of there.

"On the count of three," says Katherine. "One, two, three . . ." And all the girls yell *nigger*. All except one.

Grace stands with her head down. She hasn't called me nigger — not even for an invitation to Katherine's Halloween party.

Nobody here at school has called me that terrible name until now. I've wondered since the first day of school how long it would take and who would be the first. I always figured it'd be Grace. She and her brothers have called J.J. and me that awful name hundreds of times before. But not today.

On the way home, Grace skips to catch up with me.

"Thanks for not joining in the name-calling," I say, trying to be nice.

"Thanks for not joining them against me," she says.

"How'd you know?" I ask.

She shrugs.

"You should stop shrugging. It makes you look dumb," I say, repeating Mama's scolding.

"Dumb?" Grace shouts. "I'm just as smart as you!"

"Hey, I'm not using dumb as in *stupid*. I'm using dumb as in *mute*. When you shrug, you appear to be dumb."

"Oh," says Grace, dropping her head. Then she shifts the conversation. "What's your Halloween costume going to be?"

I'm remembering last Halloween at Attucks. Mrs. Washington suggested we dress up as a famous person in history. Then we each had to write a report about who we were. "I don't know yet. I was Phillis Wheatley last year," I tell Grace.

"Isn't that the name of the colored YWCA over on Foster Street?"

"Right. Phillis Wheatley was a very famous colored writer. I chose her because I want to be a writer one day myself."

"A colored writer?" Grace looks surprised. Then she laughs. "Come on, Rosemary, you know colored people can't write books."

Anger spews out of me like a fountain. "Now that's real dumb, as in really, really stupid!" I shout back.

"You don't know everything!"

"I know enough to be sure that you're crazy if you believe that colored people have never written books and never will." I walk ahead of her, turning to add, "That's real off in the head."

"You must hate me," Grace calls.

"No, Grace, I don't hate you. It's just hard to like you!"

"Do I need to stitch up a costume?" Mama asks.

Nothing comes to mind right away. Then I decide to do what I did last year. "I want to be Harriet Tubman. She's a famous person!"

Mama loves the idea. While she's sewing, I listen to the radio. It's a concert at Carnegie Hall in New York. I close my eyes and imagine I am there.

Mama uses an old skirt to make a new one for me. Then she pieces together a vest, an overblouse, and a big straw hat. My costume is ready. "All I have to do now is put icing on the cupcakes."

"Who are you?" Billy asks when he sees me. He's a mummy. He tries to guess. "A beggar or a ragpicker?"

"I'm Harriet Tubman," I say proudly.

He's never heard of her. Neither has Howie or Stuart. Nobody seems to know who Harriet Tubman is.

After lunch, Mrs. Denapolis realizes that there isn't going to be much work done today, so she starts the party early. "I'm going to play music and I want you to march around the room so we can all see one another's costumes," she says.

There's a ballerina, a big pumpkin, a soldier, three ghosts, three vampires, and a host of other creatures. Grace is an Indian princess. Katherine is a fairy princess. Wouldn't you know? She's been fluttering around all day, hitting people on the head with her magic wand.

"Who are you, Rosemary?" asks Mrs. Denapolis, biting into one of Mama's cupcakes. She looks so funny in a blue and red clown outfit.

"Harriet Tubman."

"Who?"

What? Mrs. Denapolis is a teacher and she doesn't know who Harriet Tubman is? I am speechless.

"Tell me," she says with no shame in her voice. "Who is she?"

So I explain who Harriet Tubman was. "The slaves called her their Moses," I say. "Because she was able to help so many of them run away to freedom in Canada."

"Is that a true story?" Katherine asks.

"Yes," I am about to answer, but before I can get it out of my mouth, Katherine jumps in.

"Why haven't we ever heard about this woman, if she's such a hero?" She waves her wand as if to dismiss me and my story.

Suddenly, Grace is on her feet. "You don't know everything," Grace says, challenging Katherine openly for the first time.

If looks could kill, we'd visit Grace every Memorial Day, at Oak Park Cemetery. Katherine and Grace have squared off. The main event could start any moment.

Mrs. Denapolis suggests that I write a paragraph about my costume character. "And I'll submit it for the *Friday Take-home*."

Mrs. Noble's first graders judge our costumes and in the end everybody is a winner and takes home a prize.

On Friday, my paragraph about Harriet Tubman is in the *Friday Take-home*. I'm a published author. The *Friday Take-home* is just a one-page sheet that keeps parents informed about various school activities, programs, projects, and general school news.

Mama shows it off to all her clients. And Mr. Bob posts a copy of it on the store window for all his customers to see and read.

Grace catches up with me on my way home as she does most days now, coming and going to school.

We walk in silence for awhile.

"Whatever happened to that cat we saw at your father's garage?" she asks. I'm impressed that she remembers.

"She's doing pretty good, I guess. Her wounds have healed, but she still doesn't meow or purr or make a sound. Would you like to see her?"

Grace smiles. "I sure would. When?"

"Now. She stays in her box most of the time out in the garage."

When we get to my house, I take Grace back to our garage. "She's over here." Daddy's got the place full of every kind of tool and car part imaginable, but there's room for Rags and her box.

Rags enjoys the attention and Grace is genuinely excited to pet her. "I love cats," she says. "I wish I had one. But it couldn't stay in the house. Mama wouldn't let it."

"Too high-minded," we say simultaneously. Then we giggle. Our mothers think alike when it comes to cats. Rags hops back into her box and curls herself into a ball.

"I feel sorry for her," I say. "Rags can't run. She can't even meow or purr like a regular cat. I guess she got too banged up."

"Or maybe she's just scared to try."

"You think so?"

"I get scared sometimes of trying new things, thinking new thoughts. You know what I mean?"

Strangely enough I did understand. At that moment, Grace doesn't seem so bad to me. And that *was* a scary thought.

CHAPTER SEVEN

Two Steps Forward — One Giant Step Back

November 1954

Sometimes I feel like I take two steps forward and one giant step back.

It's Monday morning and my fever has still not broken. Mama has called Dr. Jamison, because she thinks I might have polio.

It started Saturday evening with a sore throat. I couldn't finish eating, and midway through listening to *The Shadow*, Mama knew something was wrong when I started shaking. I don't ever remember having chills so awful. Then I stayed in bed all day Sunday, too.

"A high fever and chills are the symptoms of a lot of things, from the common cold to polio," says Dr. Jamison. "If Rosemary had any of the other symptoms — stiff neck, muscle pain, weakness, then I'd be worried."

Dr. Jamison checks me from head to toe, just to be sure. Turns out to be nothing more than a bad head cold.

"Better safe than sorry," Mama says after the doctor leaves. She tucks me into bed like she did when I was younger. All day I've been smelling her chicken and rice soup. It's almost worth getting sick to get some of it.

Daddy stops by later. I turn toward the wall and pretend to be asleep. I don't want to talk to him. I know he is cheating on mama. It's no secret anymore that he and Miss Jean are a hot item.

"She's awake, but she won't speak to me," I hear him tell Mama. "Rosemary wouldn't do that unless you've been telling her things to turn her against me."

"I resent that," Mama says. "Listen to how you sound. Rosemary is not a baby. She can see what's going on. Hear people talking. I don't need to tell her a thing."

Daddy leaves. I'm glad. No I'm not!

I convince Mama that I feel good enough to go to school on Wednesday. First thing, Katherine starts making wisecracks. "We thought you had dropped out of school."

Katherine and her stooges make it hard to be good, kind, wise, and all that other stuff Mr. Bob is always talking about. I want to tell her to go jump in the lake, but instead I ignore her. That seems to work best.

"We missed you, Rosemary. Welcome back. Hope you feel better," says Veronica.

Veronica Taylor looks more like a first-grader than a sixth-grader. She's not in Katherine's clique, either, but she doesn't seem to care.

"Thank you, Veronica," I say.

Mrs. Denapolis gives me makeup work which I complete by noon. After lunch we have a tornado drill. When the bell rings, we crawl under our desks and cover our faces. Suddenly my stomach flip-flops. It may be the medicine that's making me queasy.

I'd ask to go to Mrs. Parker, the school nurse, but she's only at school on Thursdays and Fridays.

My head is spinning and my stomach is heaving. I head for the door, but it's too late. I toss my cookies . . . and then I throw up again. All I hear behind me are *ughs*, *ags*, and *yucks*. If I could die, I'd end it all. It's easier now just to run.

I'm thinking back to first grade at Attucks, when Barbara Jean Galway threw up in class and we never let her forget it. I called her Barfa Jean, never once thinking how it might make her feel. She moved away in the fifth grade, but we were still calling her Barfa Jean. Now I'm a Barfa Jean and these kids aren't going to ever let me forget either.

Mrs. Denapolis comes into the bathroom to help me clean up.

"I'm sorry I made a mess," I whisper.

"Don't worry. The janitor is coming to clean up. I think you might have come back to school too soon," she says, touching my head. Mercifully, she decides to send me home. Good. I don't have to go back into that classroom.

Mama reads the note that Mrs. Denapolis sent explaining why I was sent home early. "For goodness sake," Mama exclaims. "Let's get you back in bed. No more of this drugstore medicine. We're going to use an old Southern remedy my mother used. It's guaranteed to work." Mama rubs my chest and temples with Vick's Salve and covers me with a warm towel. I change into flannel pajamas and cover up in a quilt.

Come morning, I'm breathing and feeling a whole lot better.

All healthy again and back in class, I'm hoping most of the kids have forgotten about the throwing up incident.

Not my luck. Everybody's been teasing me about it all day. But I found out something. Katherine the Great Mouth threw up in second grade, so she can't lead the attack. It's mostly coming from the boys, who love yucky stuff, anyway.

"Hey, Rosemary, don't eat too much, you might toss your salad again," says Howie. I stick my tongue out at him.

"Here's a riddle," says Stuart. "What's green out, green in, green on the floor?"

"What?"

"It's Rosemary! First there are green peas on her plate. The green peas go into her stomach. And then they come out again as green vomit on the floor!"

Everybody laughs. I give Stuart a dirty look. "Okay, well, then get this one. Wrapped once. Wrapped twice. Wrapped up forever."

"What's that supposed to mean?"

I stand toe to toe with Stuart. "You had a broken leg in a cast — wrapped once. You're out of the cast now, but you're fixin' to get another broken leg and cast. Wrapped twice. And if you keep messin' with me, you'll be a mummy, Stuart, wrapped up for good!"

"Very clever, Rosemary, but you don't scare me. A tiger chasing me through the jungles of Africa might scare me, but not you," Stuart says, looking around to make sure he has an audience.

"It would scare me, too," I say with a smirk. "'Cause there ain't no tigers in Africa."

"Are, too."

"Ain't! Tigers live in Asia."

"How do you know?"

"I read it in a book!"

"I know there are tigers in Africa, 'cause I saw one in a Tarzan movie."

Baloney!

"Tell you what," I say, knowing I am right on this, because Mrs. Washington taught us this last year. "Stuart, I will kiss the bottom of your shoe if I'm wrong. But then you have to kiss the bottom of my shoe if you're wrong about this."

Howie puts in quickly. "She don't know what she's talking about. Take the dare so we can see a girl kiss your shoe."

By now, a good-sized crowd is gathering. They think it's a fist-fight getting ready to explode.

"Okay," says Stuart. "How do we prove this?"

"Encyclopedia."

We run over each other getting back to class. Scurrying to the cabinet where the World Book is stored, we find a "T" and quickly turn to *Tiger*. Stuart reads the first sentence and goes pale. "Tigers are Asiatic members of the cat family. . . ."

I'll give Stuart credit, he didn't go back on his word. In front of the whole class that had gathered to see the unimaginable, a rich white boy is about to kiss the bottom of my shoe. But I stop him. "It's not necessary. I just wanted to prove that I am right, and I have! That's good enough for me," I say.

I can see Stuart's body relax.

"You're okay with me, Rosemary," he says as he walks away. Then he comes back. "One day I will go to Africa and see for myself what's there."

Somehow I feel like Simon Says I can take two big steps forward.

An amazing thing just happened. Stuart, Billy, and Grant ask me to play on their baseball team. "You're the fastest runner we've got in sixth grade. We can take on the fifth grade if you play with us. Say you will," Stuart says.

My heart is beating, so I want to jump up and down and shout yes, yes, yes. But I make myself sit still. "I'll think about it," I say.

"How long?"

"Come on, she's not gonna do it. She's a girl."

"I've finished thinking about it," I say. "Let's play ball."

Then to my surprise, they also ask Grace to join them. I know why they want me, but why her?

"She's a power hitter," says Billy.

"I play with my brothers all the time, so I have to keep up or get run over," Grace explains.

Go figure this one, if you can. Grace and I are members of the sixth-grade–recess baseball team. No other girls have ever been asked to join the team before. Talk about a giant step forward.

At recess, Mrs. Denapolis calls us together to pose for a class picture. She's using the bare trees as a background. "It reminds me of black lace on gray velvet," she says. We're all curious about her fancy camera. It's the kind professionals use.

"Are you a photographer, too?" Billy asks, watching her every move.

"It's a hobby," she says. "I will develop this picture and we can put it on the bulletin board and maybe even send one to J.J."

"I've always liked picture taking," Billy says. "Maybe we can have a camera club. What do you think?"

Mrs. Denapolis loves the idea and promises to clear it with Mrs. Lancet at the next faculty meeting.

"Can girls join the camera club, too?" Veronica asks.

Billy frowns. "Well, Mrs. Denapolis is a girl — I mean, a lady-girl — so I guess it's okay. Huh, guys?"

Several of the boys nod their approval.

"Oh, goody," Veronica says, covering her mouth and giggling.

"How about you, Rosemary? Are you going to join?" Billy asks.

"I don't have a camera," I say.

"Neither do I," says Grace.

"That's okay. Use mine," Stuart puts in.

"Then *I'm* not joining," says Katherine. She flips her long, red ponytail behind her. I'd like to strangle her with it. As she struts away she calls over her shoulder. "You can join if you want to, but I'm not and neither are any of *my* friends."

"Well, I'm joining," Veronica pipes up. "I think the camera club sounds like fun." And she giggles again. As giddy as she sounds, I have to admit I like her. She is the smallest person in class, yet she seems to have the biggest heart.

November is always Open House time. And Robertson School parents have been invited to visit from six-thirty to eight P.M. The six students who were winners of the Fire Prevention Month essay contest have been selected by Mrs. Lancet to serve as hosts and hostesses for the Open House. You could have pushed

Katherine over with a straw when I won honorable mention right alongside her. And so did Grace.

Mrs. Lancet has been busy all week running about, getting everything ready. The entrance is decorated with turkeys and Pilgrims, very colorful and festive. All the halls are filled with class projects. Our winning essays are in the glass display case in the entrance lobby. I've walked by it ten times just to see my name: "Ten Steps to Keep Your House Safe from Fires" by Rosemary Patterson.

Pictures taken by the new camera club are posted all around the school. For those of us who don't have a camera, Mrs. Denapolis lets us use one of her Brownies. I took a picture of the front door with a reflection of myself in the glass. "Not bad for a beginner," Mrs. Denapolis told me.

It's on display with the caption: "A step in the right direction." I'll be sure to write and tell J.J. all about it, complete with pictures.

"Are your parents coming to Open House?" I ask Grace. On the way home she has stopped by to see Rags.

She mumbles something I don't understand.

"What?"

"Oh, nothing."

Baloney. She did say something.

Suddenly, a shadow wipes out the sun like an eclipse. When we look, up it's the Hamiltons — Jane, Stevie, Wayne, and

Marty — standing over us like buzzards. "Forevermore. Will you look at the two of them," says Snot-nosed Marty.

Here I am facing the Hamiltons with a Hamilton. That's like fighting the Devil with an imp.

"J.J.'s not gonna believe this," I say.

"I'm here and I don't believe it, either," Grace says.

Jane and Stevie step forward. "Girl, what'cha doing here? You know Daddy'll beat you bloody if he knew you was playing with *her*." He makes "her" sound like a nasty name. "Ain't you got no self-respect?"

"All I'm doing is looking at a cat," Grace argues. "You know how I love animals." Grace's hands are shaking.

"Yeah," says Snot-nosed Marty, laughing. "Especially porch monkeys like *her*."

I clinch my fist and poke out my tongue. "Shut up, garbage mouth."

"I'm telling Daddy," he threatens.

Grace chimes in right on time. "I have plenty to tell Daddy about your stealing." She hurries on. "Jane, I could tell Mama plenty about you and that Walker boy. Wayne, you're failing everything. And Stevie, do you want me to tell Daddy that you've quit school? I ain't doing nothing wrong here, so you leave me alone. You hear?"

They slink away, like phantoms in a bog, each one mumbling something ugly.

I'm amazed at how well Grace stands up to her older siblings. I couldn't have handled the Hamiltons any better myself. Then I remember that Grace is a Hamilton. And up until two and a half months ago she was my bitter enemy.

I guess she was thinking the same thing. "Lord 'o mercy, I've gone against family for you. Have I lost my mind?" Grace shakes her head as if to clear away a horrible thought. Then in wide-eyed amazement she declares, "If I'm wrong, then why don't I feel like I'm wrong? Does this mean we're friends?" Grace seems shocked by her own words.

"One thing about it, it's a different kind of friendship."

I know Grace would rather not have a colored friend. And I wouldn't have picked her out of a catalog, either. But here we are.

Wait until I write J.J. and tell him about *this* development.

I'm disappointed — but not surprised — that Daddy won't be coming to the Open House. He says he has to work late. Baloney.

"Does he know how important this is to me?" I ask. Mama doesn't answer. She pulls the comb through my thick hair.

"Mama, please let me wear my hair down tonight," I beg.

"What did I tell you about that? When you are older."

"All the other girls in my class wear their hair down, or at least in ponytails. I look like the movie character Heidi, or a country bumpkin, in braids!"

"*All the other girls* aren't my daughter," she says. I know when she says that the conversation is over. Tonight she fools me, though, and pulls my hair into a single ponytail and bangs.

"What about lipstick and rouge?" I ask, teasing. "I guess I'll have to be twenty-five before I can wear makeup?"

"If it was left up to me, you'd be thirty-five," Mama answers. "I want to protect you as long as I can."

"Wait until you see my grades," I say, teasing. I know my grades are good, but I'm a little like Marian Ambry. I want all A's. No B's or C's — I've got to prove that Mr. Keggley wrong.

"It takes a lot of courage to do what you're doing, Rosemary. I don't know if I could do it. Both your daddy and I are so proud of you."

"But he's not proud enough to come to Open House."

"He's busy."

"Baloney," I mumble under my breath.

"What did you say?" Mama asks.

"Better hurry."

Mama and I are among the first to get to the school. She is so pleased with the way my essay is displayed. "I've had my doubts about you coming to Robertson. But Rosemary, you seem to be adjusting very well. You're a good egg. I'll keep you and be proud to call myself your mama."

Mrs. Lancet meets us in the hallway. "It's good to see you again," Mama says.

"And you, Mrs. Patterson," Mrs. Lancet replies, smiling. "Oh, this is such a busy night, but please come in sometime when we can talk. I'd love for you to be active in developing our PTA program."

"I will," says Mama. "I will." Then to me, "Nice lady."

While Mama is meeting with Mrs. Denapolis, I am busy doing my job, greeting the parents. I see Billy Jenkins's folks. I know who Mr. Jenkins is because I've seen him pick Billy up after school.

"Hello, Mr. and Mrs. Jenkins," I say. "My name is Rosemary Patterson and I am your hostess. May I offer you some punch while you wait for your appointment? Or, please have a look around the classroom at some of our work."

"My, my," says Mr. Jenkins. "Aren't you well spoken?" As they walk away I hear him whisper, "That's encouraging. Billy might improve the way *he* speaks going to school with the likes of her."

Mama finishes her meeting. She gives me a thumbs-up and a wink. "I'm going to go tour the rest of the school," she says. "I'll meet you here at eight and we can walk home together."

Meanwhile, Grace seems nervous, the way she was in the store when her brother was getting ready to steal. Easing over to her, I ask, "What's the matter?"

"Nothing."

Then to my surprise, Grace suddenly closes her eyes as if in prayer. Praying, no doubt, that when she opens them the image she's seeing will evaporate. But no, it's still there. The Hamiltons have arrived. Oh, what an image.

Mrs. Hamilton has on a black sweater pulled over a faded pink and gray skirt and a bright pink blouse. There is a hole in the elbow that her long, slender fingers keep pulling.

Mr. Hamilton has on brown work overalls and a blue-and-white checked flannel shirt, ever so properly buttoned at the neck. He smells like he's been swimming in alcohol and tobacco, and he can hardly walk or talk without slurring.

One look at Grace says it all. She wants to die. Nobody is going over to greet the Hamiltons, so I decide to do my job. "Hi, I'm Rosemary Patterson. Welcome to our sixth-grade class. . . ."

Katherine pushes past me. "Mr. and Mrs. Hamilton, please let me show you to a chair." She's only being nice to make Grace feel as uncomfortable as possible. Mr. Hamilton is very unsteady and flops on a nearby stool, knocking over art supplies in the process.

Mrs. Denapolis has finished her conference with Howie's parents. "Oh, hello," she speaks to the Hamiltons as she waves good-bye to another family.

Not waiting until they are in private, but stumbling to the middle of the room, Mr. Hamilton says in a deep Southern drawl, "I want to know, lady, are you teaching the children — our white children — that coloreds is equal to them?"

I'm thinking that I should leave. Get out of the room. But I can't make my legs move.

"I teach my students about respect for others, tolerance. Yes, I do," Mrs. Denapolis answers. "The whole school has adopted *tolerance* as our word for the year."

I'm glad Mama is not here. I think she would transfer me to Adams quicker than I could say *horse feathers*. But I wish she was here for me to hold her hand.

The room is so still, we can hear the clock hand move from one minute to the next.

Mr. Hamilton continues. He leans on Mrs. Hamilton's shoulder. "I'm as tolerant as the next man, but I don't b'lieve nohow, no-way, that the whites and the coloreds is equals."

A million thoughts are running through my mind, but I can't seem to latch on to what I should do. So I don't do anything except remain quiet.

"This ol' Arkansas country boy can't speak all proper-like, but I'm saying what y'all know is true." His words are garbled. Mrs. Hamilton brushes a loose hair from her face. "Me and my wife," he says, "don't — and most of the people in here, I bet — don't want this inner-gration one bit."

"You don't speak for us," replies Mr. Weissman, Stuart's father.

"This is America," exclaims Veronica's mother.

"Mr. Hamilton, you have a right to your opinion," says Mrs. Denapolis. "And we have a right to ours. That's all we're teaching in here. Respect." Then taking his arm, she pleads, "Please, enough. Let me share Grace's progress with you. She's doing quite well."

People begin whispering, "Disgusting."

"What a shame."

Veronica's mother rushes over to me. She is small and petite, same as Veronica. "Ronny has told me about you. I am so sorry you had to hear all of that nonsense. Not all white people think that way."

Suddenly, I am surrounded by parents who apologize to me for Mr. Hamilton's behavior.

"Pay no attention to him or anybody who talks like him," says someone else.

I must admit, it makes me feel a lot better, until I see Grace. She is cowered in a corner, looking as pale as the living dead. Then it hits me like a falling stone. She must be feeling just as humiliated as I do.

It's a typical midwestern November night — brisk, but not cold. During the walk home, I tell Mama about Mr. and Mrs. Hamilton, and everything that was said.

"Rosemary," Mama says, walking with me arm in arm, "you are no better than anybody, but you are as good as anybody. Remember that."

"I believe it, Mama." But I'm all the time wondering, *What does Grace believe?* Now that she's gotten to know me better does she think I'm inferior? That's what counts with me. How can she believe that baloney her father is saying?

"Are you sure you don't want to transfer?"

"Mama, it gets really scary sometimes and I miss my friends a lot, but I'm making new friends. I want to stay."

"Sure?"

"Sure!"

"Step on a crack, you'll break your back," says Mama, initiating our favorite game. From that point on, we measure our steps to make sure we don't step on the cracks and dividers in the sidewalk. Before we know it, we're standing in front of Daddy's garage.

In seconds, our happy mood is shattered like a windshield in a head-on collision. Miss Jean's car is parked out front. The shop lights are off. There's a small light in the apartment above. Clearly, Daddy's not working. But more than that, he is choosing to be with Miss Jean instead of coming to Open House to see about me.

"Maybe he's gone," I say. But the truck is in its usual spot. My shoulders drop as I gasp for breath the way I do after I've raced. Mama also seems to be shrinking under the heavy weight of knowing — Mama's sad that now I know and she can no longer pretend. Daddy doesn't love her or me anymore.

I hate my father.

CHAPTER EIGHT

A Slow Healing

December 1954

Thanksgiving. Christmas. They are my favorite holidays.

We ate Thanksgiving dinner with Mama's cousin in the city. They were family but they didn't feel like it to me.

Now it's time for Christmas. I know things will not be the same without Daddy, but Mama is busy planning the Sunday school Christmas party on the 11th. For as long as I can remember, Mama has hosted the gathering at our house. Mr. Bob supplies all the food and Mama and Mrs. Georgia Mae do all the cooking.

I love decorating and fixing all the cookies and goodies. The house smells like cinnamon and nutmeg. Mama is so old-fashioned though. No decorating can take place until the house is spit-polished clean. "I wouldn't dream of putting up a Christmas tree in a house with dirty windows," she says.

Makes no sense to me. Why spend days and days cleaning for a party and the guests come and it's all messed up again?

While sitting at the breakfast table in early December, looking at the variety of hotel birds living in our tree, I ask, "May I invite a few of my friends from school?"

"Of course." Mama sounds pleased.

"Even if one of them is a Hamilton?"

"Oh, honey, you can invite her, but her folks probably won't let her come."

"I'll try anyway."

Veronica became a victim of Katherine and her flunkies today. She gets teased a lot about being small. Most of the time, she's good-natured about it.

Today, though, the joking went too far. When Veronica went in the bathroom to wash up for lunch, Katherine and her hand puppets stuffed Veronica in the bathroom trash can and put the lid on. When Grace and I came in, we pulled her out.

"Stop crying," says Grace, handing Veronica a wet towel to wipe her face. "That's what they want."

"I hate it when people say that I look like Tinker Bell or a little elf! I wish I was big enough," Veronica says, "then I'd show Katherine a thing or two."

"We like you and we're somebodies," I say.

Grace shrugs, then quickly adds, "If you want, we can be friends."

Veronica wipes her eyes and a big smile takes over her face. "Really?"

"Really. So let's go eat lunch."

All week, the three of us have been eating at the same lunch table. Today Howie, Billy, and Stuart asked to join us.

"Why?" I ask.

"'Cause you always look like you're having fun," says Stuart.

We three look at one another and smile. "Even if we're girls?"

"But you're not like girls," says Howie.

Now that's a real compliment!

"Come on then," says Veronica. "We'll tolerate you."

Katherine scowls every time she passes our table. "Losers," she sneers. Our table is a strange combination of people, sort of like birds in our hotel tree. We aren't birds of the same feather, but we're flocking together.

Gotta tell J.J. all about this. It's been a long time since I've heard from him. I'm wondering what's going on.

Divorce! People still whisper the word around me even though I'm eleven. Mama is divorcing Daddy. She has stopped looking toward the door at every sound, expecting it to be Daddy. But I haven't. A part of me — the part that still loves Daddy — listens for him to come lumbering through the house with an arm full of groceries and a face full of smiles. But the part of me that is angry with Daddy wants him to stay away.

Mama has done her best to explain the situation. "Your father and I are getting divorced. He's unhappy without me, but he is not completely happy with me. We are all miserable."

"Has he stopped loving us?"

"No. Your daddy loves you with all his heart. Don't ever misplace that thought."

"Baloney! He loves Miss Jean more than us. And I hate him just like you!"

Mama pulls me to her. "I don't hate your father. Hate is a word that cripples your spirit. Sorta like the way polio has maimed J.J. Your father and I have grown out of love. But we don't hate each other." Mama voice was stern. "I never want you to say you hate your father again. Is that clear?"

"But . . ."

"What did I say? Not another word about this. Besides," she added. "Deep down you know you love him very much."

And that ends the great talk we were supposed to have. I am more confused than ever and there is nobody else I dare ask.

Rags listens to all my worries and complaints. "I want to hate Daddy, if it would make Mama feel better. But that's not what she wants, or me, either," I say.

■ ■ ■

I invited all the lunch group to the Christmas party. All of them had something else planned. Or so they said.

On the 11th at 3:00 P.M. sharp, Grace knocks on my door. There's a light dusting of snow on the ground that makes the front yard look like it's sugarcoated. The house sparkles and glistens like new money.

"So you came?" I say.

"I bet your daddy doesn't know you're here."

Grace looks behind her. She gets all red in the face. "No, if he knew I was here, he'd skin me alive. But I slipped out and came anyway."

Mama brings out the hot dogs, potato chips, cake, and cookies for twenty kids. We wash it all down with two bowls of punch. Then we listen to records and play games.

Later, the guests leave, but Grace stays.

"I was the only white person here," Grace says, looking wide-eyed. "I felt scared at first. You know like butterflies in my stomach."

"Now you know how I feel sometimes being the only colored girl in the class."

"Yeah, but everybody was so nice. Even Estelean. And we've never gotten along."

"I put in a good word for you," I say.

"Why don't you show Grace your room?" Mama says.

When Grace gets to my bedroom door, she stops. Her eyes circle the room. "Is this yours, all by yourself?" she asks.

"Yeah, but I wouldn't mind sharing it with a sister. Not a brother, but a sister would be fine."

Grace rubs the pink, green, and white chenille bedspread. "This is so pretty. What's this around the side of the bed?"

"A dust ruffle. Mama sews, you know, so she made the curtains, too. I hide a lot of toys underneath the bed when I'm hurrying to clean up."

"More toys? You are so lucky."

"I'm an only child, Grace."

"I've never been in a colored person's house before. It's not at all what I expected. This is a palace."

I invite her to follow me into the kitchen where I cut us another piece of cake. "There are a lot of colored people with pretty houses and nice things. But we aren't rich. Mama says rich is how you feel inside, not what you wear or where you live. Come on, let's go see Rags."

She is curled in a ball, asleep as usual. "She still doesn't meow or purr, but I've been putting her out of her box until night," I explain.

"Your mama sounds like a good person," Grace says. "Mine is, too. Is your father nice?"

I am silent for a long while. "Grace, if I share a secret, will you tell?"

"Never. Cross my heart and hope to die." She moves in close and I whisper. "I let Rags sleep in the bed with me at night."

"Really!" She brushes a piece of hair out of her face, the way Mrs. Hamilton did the night of the Open House. I realize then how much Grace looks like her mother. "I promise not to tell, not even if I'm tortured and beaten to within an inch of my life, and boiled in oil. . . ."

"Okay, Grace," I say holding up my hand. "I believe you won't tell. But this is the real secret. My parents are getting a divorce."

The next day, Mama gets a letter from Aunt Betty. Mama shares some of it with me. The reason why I haven't heard from J.J. is because he's feeling way, way down.

"It was like his hopes were high, but the therapy is hard and it hurts a lot. And it isn't going as fast as he wants. He's really crushed, and Betty is worried," Mama explains.

Later, I write him a long letter.

A wheelchair is easy to sit in. It's hard to walk. I took Rags's box from her. It sounds hard, but all she was doing was sleeping. You need to get out of that wheelchair if you're ever going to run again.

Your friend,
Rosemary

Since I was a little girl, Daddy and I have gone into the city to the Cameo Movie Theater on Christmas Eve. It gives Mama time to wrap gifts and get everything finished. I don't want to go this year, but Mama insists that I meet Daddy at the garage. Right away, he tells me we aren't going to the movies. Instead, we go to the Hilltop Café, the only colored restaurant in town.

I've always wondered why they call it the Hilltop Café because it sits on a perfectly flat corner. Doesn't matter, they have the best food in town. I especially enjoy sitting on the orange-covered stools at the counter.

"Catfish sandwich on white. Hold the pickles. Hot dog and a bowl of chili." Daddy orders for us, then adds, "Rosemary, I have something to tell you. . . ."

"I know what it is already," I say, butting in. I take a seat in a booth rather than my favorite counter spot. "You and Mama are getting a divorce. You love Miss Jean and want to be with her instead of us."

I've never seen him look so angry and sad all at the same time. "Who told you that? Your mother?"

"No," I shout. "I figured it out myself. Nobody had to tell me. I saw her car at the garage the night you said you had to work and couldn't come to Open House at school."

"Look." Daddy speaks softly, sliding in next to me. "When mothers and fathers divorce, they don't divorce their children. And there is not a person in the world I love more than you. And no matter what happens between your mother and me, you are still my daughter. . . ."

Blah, blah, blah, blah. All of it sounds so fake. And I don't want to hear it. I look away.

"Okay," he says, chomping on his sandwich. "We won't talk about unpleasantries. That's between your Mama and me, anyway. Don't you worry about a thing. Besides, I don't want to spoil your surprise."

Back at the garage, Daddy fumbles for the key when suddenly the door opens.

"Well, hello, Mel-vin," says Miss Jean.

"I didn't know you were working . . . stopping by today," he says, sounding shocked and a little bit put off to see Miss Jean there.

"Well, I wanted to be a part of Rosie's big surprise. Oh, did I do the wrong thing, sugah?"

"No, no, you're welcome to stay."

I'm still standing in the doorway. I'm ready to leave, but Daddy is holding onto me and I can't get away.

"Come here, baby girl," he says, showing me a television set.

"Merry Christmas!" he shouts. Then he switches it on.

"Rosie, don't you just love it?" Miss Jean says.

"I'd like it better if you wouldn't call me Rosie. My name is Rosemary, same as my grandmother's."

Daddy is busy working with the television. "Your mother

thinks a television set is a waste of money. But it's the wave of the future, so I went out and bought one — for you."

"The television set is for me?"

Daddy starts turning knobs and buttons. Suddenly a picture comes on the screen. "I'll keep it here, of course, and you can come watch it anytime you want. Now you can see stories rather than just listening to them on the radio."

There aren't but two or three families who have televisions in our neighborhood.

"I'm ready to go home now," I say.

"Don't you like the television set?" Daddy asks. "It cost a lot of money."

"I didn't ask for it," I say. "If you were around more you'd know that what I really want is a camera. So you can keep your television set. I'll never look at it."

"Don't you smart-mouth your father, nice as he is to you," Miss Jean says. "If you were mine, I'd give you a good switching."

"But she's not yours," says Daddy. "Let me handle this." Then turning to me, he says calmly, "If you change your mind, it will be here for you to see whenever you'd like."

Merry Christmas. Bah-Humbug!

CHAPTER NINE

Small Victories

Winter 1955

1955

    A new year. A double-nickel year.

    Mr. Bob is selling eggs for twenty-seven cents.

    A bus ride to town is ten cents and a nickel for a transfer.

    The new Ford is beautiful, but who can afford one at $1600?

    And a package of notebook paper is twenty cents.

    The holidays were filled with the usual stars, lighted angels, bell-ringing, singing Santas, candied cookies, dazzling Christmas trees, and merry, merry times. Then it was all over.

    The tree comes down. The bells and stars and angels get tucked away until next year, and the merry, merry gets covered under three feet of snow.

    When we return to school in January with our new notebooks, new boxes of crayons, new shoes and sweaters, we are ready for the second half of the school year. Our lunch group shares what we got for Christmas. Stuart isn't back yet from his trip to Colorado. His family goes out every year to ski.

"Must be nice," says Veronica. "What'd you get for Christmas, Rosemary?"

"A hat and pair of mittens. A new book. My mama surprised me with a Brownie camera." I'd dropped enough hints. I'm glad she heard me. "I don't have to use Mrs. Denapolis's camera anymore."

"I got two books, a pen and pencil set, and new wallet," says Veronica.

"I got a pair of ice skates," Grace exclaims. "Want to go ice-skating over on Milton's Pond?" Everyone agrees, except me.

"At the pond and not at the club?" I dramatize in Katherine's best Bette Davis Hollywood-actress voice. We all laugh. But inside I'm thinking about ice-skating on Milton's Pond. I've picnicked there, and I've fished there. But I have never ice-skated anywhere.

"What about this Saturday? We'll all meet there," Grace says.

I hate to admit that I've never ice-skated in my life. So I pretend that I'm not interested. "Got too much to do," I say.

"You can't skate, can you?" Grace teases. "Finally! Something you can't do that I can. Well, listen. If an Arkansas hillbilly girl like me can learn to ice-skate, you can, too."

"Maybe," I answer. No sense in denying it. "You're right."

"Saturday, then?"

"Maybe."

"Say yes," she insists.

"Okay. Saturday," I say.

Three lessons and I think I'm a whiz. Already I'm making future plans.

"Who knows?" I say, attempting a slow spin. "One day I might be an Olympic champion ice-skater."

"Rosemary, you'd be the first in your race to do it, but I bet you could."

"Thanks for saying that, Grace. But you've got a far better chance than me, because you already skate like a champion. . . ."

At that moment, my feet slip and I fall flat on my bottom.

"Some Olympian!" Grace is laughing so hard, she falls, too.

We go home and have hot chocolate at my house, the way good friends do.

Actually, I've enjoyed winter more than ever before. Maybe it's because I can ice-skate now, and so can Estelean. It wasn't easy getting Estelean on blades, though.

Here's what happened:

Estelean hadn't been herself since September. She didn't laugh nearly as much. She held her head down and she rarely played.

One winter day, I finally got her to try on my ice skates and wobble around the pond. "Too hard for me," she muttered after one try. She took off the skates and tossed them back to me real hateful-like.

"Try once more," I insisted.

"Don't wanna," she said. Her voice was so small that the wind whisked it away before my ears grabbed it. I asked her to repeat it.

"We've always roller-skated together," she shouted. "Now you're ice-skating with the white girls," she snapped.

"Are you mad at me for being friends with white girls?"

"Yes! No," she answered quickly. "I don't know. I'm mad because . . . nothing is the same." She balled her hands into fists.

"Estelean, we're still friends," I said. "Come on now. If you want to learn how to skate, all you have to do is try a little harder."

Estelean's lip curled into an angry snarl. "What do you know about trying hard? Everything you do is perfect. I try, but it's never enough. Everybody says I should do more, write more, read more. Well, I do try, and nothing gets better."

Estelean wasn't talking about ice-skating anymore. And she wasn't necessarily mad at me. I was just the one closest to her anger. "What's really wrong? I really want to know."

That's when she broke down and told me how unhappy she was at Adams. Her grades were falling, and she'd been sent to the office twice for back-talking. "I got a C in math on my report card and a D for conduct and that's never, ever happened before. Foxy-Loxy is plain ol' prejudiced. I'm not the only one. She just doesn't like any of us colored kids. She treats us like we're dumb and stupid." Estelean covered her face with her hands.

I knew it was bad at Adams, but I had no idea it was as awful as Estelean described. I couldn't help but think how lucky I was to have a teacher like Mrs. Denapolis. "Maybe your teacher is another Mrs. Parker. Remember she taught at Attucks," I said, trying to console my friend.

"I remember Mrs. Parker. She was a no-nonsense teacher but she was fair. Mrs. Foxworthy is not fair. Period."

"Have you told your folks about Mrs. Foxworthy?"

"Yes. But they don't understand. They think integration is wonderful. Nobody wants to listen to our side of the story."

"I'll always listen."

"Really? How come?"

It is so like Estelean to ask questions like that. "Because you are my friend," I answer.

"Why do you call me friend, instead of *best friend*? Are Grace and Veronica your best friends now?"

"Is that what this is all about?" I answered carefully. "All of you are my friends."

"But which one of us is your best friend?"

I knew what Estelean wanted to hear, but I answered truthfully. "J.J. is my best friend."

"What? A boy can't be a girl's best friend."

"Who says so?"

Estelean thought about it for a minute. "That's okay by me!" She dried her eyes and perked up some. "J.J.'s your best *boy* friend. Then I can be your best *girl* friend."

"If you say so, Estelean." That's fine with me, too.

We sat in silence for awhile, pondering what we'd shared. With a deep sigh, Estelean whispered more to herself than me. "Mama says I have to keep on trying no matter how hard it gets. So I will." Then with a half-smile, she turned to me. "Well, Rosemary, are you gonna teach your best friend to skate or not?"

"You bet!"

Estelean tries hard, and though it takes awhile, she learns how to ice-skate. And let me tell you, she's good! Nobody can deny her that claim to fame. When she's on the ice, she takes off her glasses, throws back her head, and spins like a top. She's just small enough to be quick and agile as she sails around the pond, first gliding, then leaping. Her whole body seems happy, but the wide grin on her face tells it all. Estelean feels like a winner. Who knows? Maybe one day *she* will be the Olympian!

■   ■   ■

Sunday, I see my friends from Attucks after church — Kevin, Gabe, and the others. Mama made me sit beside her, so I couldn't talk.

"Have you heard?" Estelean tells me afterward. "Flora's Mama is sending her down south where the schools are still segregated."

"When?" I ask.

"Next week."

"And did you hear about Bevvy?" Estelean lowers her voice to a whisper. "She's big."

"What?"

Estelean looks at me as if I'm an idiot. "She swallowed a pumpkin seed."

"Are you trying to say she's pregnant?" I ask, forthright.

"Shhhhh! Don't say it so loud." She is more birdy than ever.

I feel awful for Bevvy. She's supposed to graduate in June and go to secretarial school. I guess she can forget about that now.

"She and Tommy Lee are getting married next Sunday after church," says Estelean, filling in the details.

"I never want to get married," I say, without explaining why. It's hard to believe I have told Grace about the divorce but not Estelean.

It's cold, colder than it should be at this time of year. It's supposed to drop down in the twenties before morning. Mama let Rags stay in my room. But she would have a fit if she knew that I let Rags sleep in my bed.

"We can't get caught," I whisper to her.

"Meow," she answers, and curls her body in a ball by my side, closes her eyes, and purrs like a new Ford motor. "Wait 'til I write and tell J.J. that you have finally made a sound," I say, laughing. Rags is talking!

Got a letter from J.J. with a picture in it. He's sitting in a drum full of bubbling water next to his therapist and doctor.

Dear Rosemary,

Sorry I have not written. I guess I've been too busy and sore to say much. I love getting your letters. Sounds like a lot is going on.

The water treatments are long and hard. When the therapist massages my legs, it hurts so badly I can hardly stand it. I try not to scream out, but sometimes I can't help it.

I don't want to stay here always. So, I won't give up. Thanks for reminding me about Rags, and warning me about the wheelchair.

So you and Grace the Tasteless are friends now. I guess I'm okay with that.

Mama worries too much. Tell Aunt Doris and Uncle Mel hello. Bootsie and Josh are growing like crazy. Daddy came down a week ago. He looks tired. I'll be so glad when this is over.

Your best friend always,

J.J.

A knock at the door is frightening at any late-night hour. But the knock at our door is loud. It is a bitter cold February morning, though it is not light outside yet.

"Mrs. Patterson, please, open up. Please."

I recognize Grace's voice. Pulling on my robe, Mama and I get to the door at the same time. "What in the world?" Mama asks.

"It's Ma. She's very sick, burning hot with fever." Grace is near panic. "Jane and I have tried everything, but nothing helps. Will you please come?" Grace looks wild with fear and anxiety.

"Where are your father and brothers? Wouldn't it be better to get your mother to call a doctor?" Mama asks, still trying to grasp the urgency.

"Daddy's working a double shift at the steel mill, and my two older brothers aren't at home anymore. Please hurry," Grace pleads.

Mama and I quickly dress and hurry through the early morning dew to the Hamiltons' yard and into the house. "You know Pops wouldn't want them in here," Jane whispers.

"Shut up." Grace snaps at her sister. "Ma needs help."

Grace leads us to Mrs. Hamilton, who is lying in bed. She is burning with fever and moaning softly. Mama begins barking orders like a nurse. "Get me a bowl of warm water and a wash towel," Mama says. Jane refuses to obey. "You'd better mind me, girl," Mama says in her no-nonsense voice. Jane scurries toward the bathroom.

I watch as Mama gives Mrs. Hamilton the same treatment she gives me when I have a fever. First, she rubs Vick's Salve on Mrs. Hamilton's chest, then covers her in a blanket warmed over the coal stove. Nothing to do now but wait.

By late afternoon, her fever breaks, and she is able to swallow a few tablespoons of the chicken and rice soup Mama has made.

Then all of a sudden, the front door flies open. "Woman," Mr. Hamilton yells as he comes in. "I'm home. Something sure smells good."

Mr. Hamilton stops short when he sees Mama sitting beside Mrs. Hamilton. "What . . ." He looks to Jane for an explanation. She shrugs. I promise myself that I'll never shrug again. Jane looks dumb — as in mute — but also dumb as in stupid.

Mrs. Hamilton raises up on one elbow. She is still very weak. "I'm beholden to this fine lady for seeing after me, and by God I want her treated right in this house, do you hear me?" She coughs and falls back on her pillow.

Mr. Hamilton gives a weak grunt, then walks away. Mama makes sure Mrs. Hamilton is okay. Then we leave quietly.

Our sixth-grade lunch table is growing daily. Lots of kids sit with us now. We talk, trade cards, and compare notes on sports figures, movies, and games.

Today, Grace seems moody, standoffish.

We have indoor recess, so I sit with her high in the bleachers where we can talk privately. "I bet your father flipped his switch when we left," I say.

Grace covers her face with her hand. "My father's a good man," she says, sounding defensive. I've heard this tone in her voice before. "Pop works hard and does what a good father should do. And I love him in spite of how awful he can be."

"I love-hate my father in the same way," I reply.

"No, Rosemary," she counters. "My father is nothing like yours. Believe me."

That's when I notice a bruise on her lower arm. "Did he beat you?"

"No! No!" she says. "He's a good father who wants us to be obedient. I haven't been very obedient. . . ."

"Being friends with me? Is that why he punished you? Why does he hate colored people so much?" I find the courage to ask after all these months.

Grace doesn't answer. "Pop honestly thinks that white people are superior to colored people. I can't change his mind. Nobody can."

I think about that. "You know better, don't you?"

"Now I do."

"That's what counts with me."

We lapse into silence, as we often do, until I find the words to say what I mean. "Grace, if being my friend causes you to get into trouble with your folks, then maybe we should stop being friends."

Grace touches my hand and pulls it back.

"The color doesn't rub off," I say.

"I know. I didn't know if you wanted me to touch you. I touched Katherine one day and she acted like I had cooties or some bad disease."

"That girl is a puzzle with pieces missing — hard to play with and not much fun," I say.

That makes Grace smile. "If you want to still be my friend, then I still want to be yours."

"But what about your father?"

"I'm going to start with my ma first," she says. "She's the only person in the world who can handle my dad. If I can convince her to let us be friends, then Pops will go along with her."

A few nights later, after dinner, there is a knock at the door. To our surprise, it is Mrs. Hamilton and Grace.

"How do?" says Mrs. Hamilton. Her lips are drawn tight. I could see this is not easy for her.

"Come in." Mama graciously welcomes them. "How are you feeling, Mrs. Hamilton? I hope you aren't up and about too soon."

She is reluctant to come inside, but Grace pulls her mother into the house. "See, Mama. Just like I told you. It's beautiful."

Mama offers them chairs, but Mrs. Hamilton declines. She refuses Mama's offer of coffee or tea, too.

"We won't be long," she says, and starts right in with why she has come. "I'm a simple woman from Arkansas, brought up with ideas that are hard to toss aside. But I ain't as ignorant as some of my own flesh and blood think I am." She looks at Grace who drops her head. "I do know how to say thank you. Thank you for helping me when I was in need."

Now I figure this is about all Mrs. Hamilton is able to give, considering her attitudes are the same as her husband's.

"I brung this vinegar pie," she says, "to say thank you again. I wrote on the bottom the story behind where the recipe comes from."

Mama accepts the pie the way one might receive a package from the mailman.

"And one more thing," Mrs. Hamilton adds. "Our young'un seem to have taken a liking for each other. Fancy they is friends." Grace and I find each other's eyes. "Well, I wasn't much on it, but I can see how happy my baby is. I can also see you're a good Christian woman, like myself. And I'm 'bliged to give my permission for them to be friends, if you are of like mind."

"Well," says Mama, "I'm particular about who Rosemary keeps company with. But I think the girls will appreciate knowing that they have our approval."

■   ■   ■

When they are gone, Mama and I say at the same time, "Vinegar pie!" Makes me want to gag. Mama and I take the pie to the kitchen and stare at it as if it is going to attack us. "Is it edible?" I ask, giggling.

Mama opens the note and reads. "Says here it's an old recipe that pioneer women made in the winter when fresh fruits weren't available for pies. Here's the recipe:

4 EGGS

1 $\frac{1}{2}$ CUPS SUGAR

1 TEASPOON VANILLA

$\frac{1}{2}$ STICK MELTED BUTTER

1 $\frac{1}{2}$ TABLESPOONS APPLE CIDER VINEGAR

MIX ALL THE INGREDIENTS UNTIL SMOOTH AND CREAMY. POUR INTO AN 8-INCH PIE SHELL. BAKE AT 350 DEGREES FOR 40 MINUTES.

"Nothing in it that's not good," Mama says. "Let's see what it tastes like." She cuts a slice for the two of us.

"I bet it's gonna be nasty."

Man 'o man, am I wrong!

It's delicious! It's as good as Mama's chess pie, though I'd never tell her.

"I guess we're all a little bit prejudiced, huh, Mama?"

"But it's never too late to learn."

"Look at what we'd be missing if we hadn't tried it."

Later, when Mama comes in to check on me before bed, she sits on the side of my bed. "It's the little victories that win the war," she says on her way out the door. "Tell Rags I hope she sleeps soundly. . . in your bed!"

Mrs. Denapolis has convinced several of us to enter the upcoming district-wide Mid-Winter Spelling Bee on Monday, February 21. All the information is posted on the bulletin board. I read it, but I'm not sure.

"I'm no good in spelling," says Howie.

"Me, neither," Billy puts in.

"How about you, Rosemary?" Howie asks.

"She wouldn't have a chance," Katherine says.

That's the clincher! I decide then and there to enter the competition.

When I get home from school today, there is a letter from J.J. It seems the treatments are going better than expected. Only one leg will have to be in a brace. But the best news of all is that Mrs. Washington visited him.

. . . Remember? She attends Fisk, which is across the street from Meharry Hospital. Mama met her in the hallway one day. She came to see me and now

she is working with me and a few other kids on our schoolwork until we can go to regular school. You'd be happy to know I am a much better student now than I was. I can't do much of anything but read and write. So in a way, Mrs. Washington did start her own school. . . . She sends her best, Madam President. With all the bad stuff that is happening, I really feel lucky to have Mrs. Washington.

Your best friend,
J.J.

P.S. My therapist took my wheelchair away. Like you said it was the best thing that ever happened to me. It made me walk. It is just like when you took Rags out of her box and threw it away. Then she was forced to use her legs.

So here I am in the high school auditorium. I've made it all the way to the finals of the spelling bee. There are only two other colored kids who have made it this far. I know them both. Jason is in sixth grade at Adams. We go to church together. The other colored kid is Percy, a fifth-grader, who beat out his twin to make it to the finals.

Mr. Keggley is the moderator, giving out the words. Of all people. I know he's dismayed that his tests were all wrong. I am doing so much better than he ever would have expected.

Katherine and I represent Robertson's fifth–sixth-grade level. Mrs. Lancet and Mrs. Denapolis are in the audience. Mama is sitting third row, center. I found her has soon as I came onstage. I don't see Daddy. I wonder if he's here.

Round after round, we're challenged with words: *formula, grotesque, gymnasium, convertible*. When I'm not sure, I guess, remembering the rules Mrs. Washington and Mrs. Denapolis have taught. So far, I manage to guess correctly. One by one, participants are eliminated. Katherine holds on, because for all the meanness she's also a very good student. She's been given the word *strategy*. She stands up. "Strategy." She pronounces the word. Then she says each letter slowly. "S-T-R-A-D-E-G-Y. Strategy."

The gong sounds. "Incorrect!" announces Mr. Keggley. Katherine is a sore loser. She flops in her seat, folds her arms, and scowls.

Jason is taken out by a simple word, *calendar*, and Percy gets jammed by *discipline*.

Now it's down to two contestants — a fifth-grader from Adams and me.

At some point, Daddy has eased in and is sitting behind Mama. I like seeing them together, even if they aren't *together*.

Katherine leans over to me. "It's up to you, Rosemary," she whispers in passing. "You'd better win!"

Wilson McDonald, the finalist from Adams, is asked to spell *anxiety*. He zips it off easily.

"Correct," says Mr. Keggley. Then turning to me he speaks extra slowly and distinctly. "Rosemary, spell *extrapolate*."

Extrapolate? I've never seen or heard the word. Mr. Keggley defines it, but that's no help. Nervously, I begin to call letters. My mouth feels like it's filled with cotton. E-X-T-R-A-P-A-L-A-T-E. The gong sounds. "Wrong answer," says Mr. Keggley, almost joyfully.

"Wilson, if you spell your next word correctly then you will be our 1955 Spelling Bee champion! Spell *appendix*." Then he defines it.

Once again, Wilson zips off the letters and wins the contest.

Mr. Keggley is obviously delighted to give Wilson the four Cardinal baseball tickets. I feel like I've been mugged and left to bleed to death by the side of the road. I've lost for myself, my parents, my school, and my race. *Extrapolate* — a word I'll always remember, even if I can't spell it.

The hard part about losing is standing onstage, watching your opponent take the first-place prize. I've learned something about myself. I don't like to lose. Daddy says I get it from Mama. Losing brings out the worst in me, no matter how hard I try to push the ugly behavior back.

"And now for second place," says Mr. Keggley. "For Miss Rosemary Patterson, a fine representative of her race, we have a gift certificate to the Hawthorne House Restaurant, one of the finest in the city."

And he forgets to say it's also segregated. Mama is furious. Her eyes are unnaturally dark. Her hands are clutching her gloves as if she means to strangle them. She complains to Mr. Keggley about the gift certificate. I only hear bits and pieces. "How . . . so insensitive? She's a child, forget about our differences . . . unfair . . ."

Mrs. Lancet is likewise livid. She has words with Mr. Keggley. So does Mrs. Denapolis. Even when Daddy tries to reason with Mr. Keggley, he turns a deaf ear. Daddy walks away to keep from losing his temper.

For all their efforts, they can't change the situation. Mr. Keggley was prejudiced when assigning the words, and it is obvious he didn't expect anybody colored to win the contest. Now I have won a useless certificate to a segregated restaurant as a prize.

The next day after Mama has cooled down, she suggests that I give the gift certificate to Mrs. Denapolis. "She has been so thoughtful and considerate. Let her have a night out with her husband."

When I tell Mr. Bob the story, he gives his usual advice. "Don't let petty prejudices like this undermine your self-confidence. You did your best and that's what counts. There is no shame in being runner-up."

At lunch, though, Katherine comes striding over to our table. "I think the whole spelling bee thing stinks," she says.

I'm thinking that's all I need, is more chatter from her. "Look, Katherine . . ."

"No, you look," she interrupts. "My father knows the owner of the Hawthorne. I'm going to tell him about the gift certificate.

Rosemary, you won that contest, hands down. A first-grader could spell *appendix*. But *extrapolate* is a college word. I don't like to lose, but when it's not fair, then I get even. You're going to the Hawthorne."

And with a flip of her red braids, she struts away.

"Who's her dad?" Grace asks.

"Bruce Hogan, a big-time lawyer," Stuart replies.

"Isn't that nice of Katherine to do this for you," says Grace.

"*Me!* Katherine isn't doing this for me. Katherine wanted *her* class, *her* school, to win the spelling bee. When Mr. Keggley stole the championship from me, Katherine took it personally."

Whatever her reason, true to her word, Katherine's father uses his influence to get the Hawthorne to make good on the gift certificate.

I redeem my coupon on a Wednesday evening in February. It's a tasty meal, elegantly prepared, complete with violins, but served in an empty restaurant, save Mama and me.

Mama makes sure that I write a thank-you note to Mr. Hogan. One of the ladies who gets her hair fixed at Miz Lilly Belle's does the Hogans' laundry. She told Mama that Bruce Hogan is a new partner in the Lomar, Brooks, and Allen law firm. He's handling all the civil rights cases.

Just when you think you've got it all figured out, something happens to confuse you all over again. Who would have guessed that Katherine's father was one of the lawyers who helped lead the fight to integrate Kirkland schools?

"I'm not surprised Bruce Hogan helped. He handles all my legal affairs," Mr. Bob told me. "He's a friend of our people. Say, he has a daughter about your age, doesn't he?"

"Yes, sir. Katherine," I answer, trying not to show my astonishment. "She's in my class."

"If she's anything like her father, she must be a very nice person," Mr. Bob says, stacking canned peaches.

I decide not to answer.

Daddy arrives shortly after school is out on Friday to take me to our promised dinner at Hilltop.

Daddy looks tired. There are big circles under his eyes. He thumps his fingers on the table nervously. "How's Miss Jean?" I ask.

"Who knows? She's gone back to Kentucky."

"She's gone!" I try not to act too happy about it.

Daddy moves in close so our conversation is private. "Baby girl, does your mother talk about me — like in a good way?"

"She doesn't say anything about you to me. Only when you are coming by and when I am to be ready. Nothing more."

"I think I've made a big mistake," he says. "A super-duper, stupid mistake!"

A few days later, Daddy brings the television to our house.

Mama doesn't want it. "It's ugly," she says. "And it will be in the way."

"Look, television is the wave of the future. Don't deny Rosemary that. Anyway, a half million people can't be wrong."

"Now you listen, Melvin. I don't do things because everybody else is. Think about . . ."

"I know, I'm too impulsive." He throws his arms in the air, then lets them drop to his sides. "Let's not fight. Not over a gift. I'm giving the television set to my daughter as a gift. Will you get out of the way and let her have it?"

In the end, he convinces Mama. She lets me keep the TV.

TV is short for "television." That's what people are beginning to call it.

Wait until I write J.J. and tell him I just watched *The Adventures of the Lone Ranger* on TV.

CHAPTER TEN

A Different Kind of Friendship

March. April. May.

Winter snows are over. Ice on the pond has melted. No more snowball fights or sledding or ice-skating.

The apple tree out back is in full bloom. The blossoms look like a white cloud has enveloped us here on the ground. Surrounded by all this color and beauty, my mood is gray. I feel bored! But Rags is busy batting at a passing butterfly.

When I evicted Rags from her box, she transformed into an amazing cat, running and stalking everything from birds to dogs. Actually, she gets around on three legs better than most whole cats. "You're a wild thing," I tell her. "Wait 'til I tell J.J. you're running!"

Dear J.J.,

   Rags is not only running, she is climbing trees with just three legs! Tell Mrs. Washington hello.

Your best friend,
Rosemary

P.S. Hurry home so we can watch "Hopalong-Cassidy" together.

Estelean wasn't the only person who has had a hard winter. It's been no piece of cake for me, either. Mama's lawyer tells her a court date has been set for her divorce. When Daddy gets the papers, he comes by the house in a fit. Of course, I'm sent to my room, as if they're going to say something I don't already know. Rags settles in my lap while I listen at the door. Daddy is easy to hear.

"You can't throw away our years together," he shouts, pacing the floor like a caged cat.

"Oh, Mel, I didn't throw us away. You did," Mama says.

"That girl is to blame," he snapped back. "She played me like a bass fiddle. Now she's gone — gone back to Kentucky. I wish I'd never laid eyes on her." Thank goodness. Daddy finally has come to his senses, I'm thinking. But Mama isn't moving.

Mama's voice grows cold. "So nothing is your fault?"

"Women expect men to be perfect. That's the problem."

I'm thinking Daddy shouldn't have said that.

"No," Mama says. "Your attitude *about* women is your problem."

"You know what your problem is?" he says. "You're too independent."

Everything is silent.

Mama sighs, but I can hear the stiffness in her voice when she says, "We're not right for each other. Please, just go."

Daddy refuses to give up. "You want me to beg — fall on my face and beg? Is that it? You want to see me cry like a schoolboy? Okay. I will. Tell me what you need."

Mama slowly and deliberately replies. "I want you to leave. Just go."

No, Mama. She can't be sending him away. I hoped for so long that he would come back to us. Now that he has Mama is making him go. "Adults are too hard to understand," I tell Rags.

When Daddy leaves, the house is quiet. No ball game is playing. No TV. No arguments. I hear the low hum of our refrigerator and the steady tick-tock of the hall clock. It is only five o'clock in the evening, but it seems later. I hear Mama softly sobbing. I hold Rags close and cry, too. I know now for sure, the marriage is over.

Later, at the dinner table, Mama is pushing food from one side of her plate to the other. Neither one of us is hungry. I finally get the nerve to tell Mama my feelings. "Daddy loves you," I say, stabbing at my corn. "He's the same daddy he's always been," I argue.

"That's it exactly. He is the same daddy."

I push my plate away. The food tastes like straw. "Now that Miss Jean is gone, why can't you two get back together?"

Mama puts her hand over my hand. Her eyes are soft, though dark. "Miss Jean is not the main reason for our breakup. Your father and I have been growing apart for some time. We are different people than we were when we first got married. And our differences make it impossible for us to stay together."

"But you're giving up, Mama. J.J. hasn't given up. Rags hasn't given up. I haven't given up either. Please don't give up on Daddy. He said he was sorry."

Mama studied my face for a long time. "There is no way to make you understand this now," she says. "But one day you will. I'm not giving up. I'm moving on."

Grabbing a glass of milk and a cookie, I hurry to meet Estelean, Grace, and Veronica out by the apple tree and share J.J.'s latest letter with them.

"What's the matter with Rags?" Grace asks.

I examine her from head to toe to make sure she hasn't hurt herself again. "I don't know."

"She's huge and lumpy!" says Estelean.

Satisfied that she's okay, I answer, "Rags is not fat; she is well-fed and pleasingly plump. That's all."

Grace turns up her nose. "She's fat!"

"Sure is," Veronica agrees.

After looking at Rags from another angle, I have to agree. "She *is* fat."

"Are you going to the Spring Garden Concert?" Estelean asks. I shrug.

"Don't look dumb," Grace says, teasing. Veronica giggles.

The Spring Garden Concert is a special event in the Kirkland community. All the girls from every school dress up in beautiful dresses made of soft fabric such as chiffon, lace, or organdy. The boys wear suits and ties. They assemble at the botanical gardens to listen to an outdoor concert presented by the St. Louis Symphony Orchestra. It's also a contest for all music students. Several students are selected by the music director to play a piece with the orchestra. "I'm not musical one bit, but I'm looking forward to attending this year," I say.

"I'm not going," Grace announces.

"Why not?" Veronica puts in.

"Why is it so important to attend everything that's going on?" she answers in that sullen tone she takes when she's embarrassed about something.

"What's the matter, you don't have anything glamorous to wear?" The moment I say it, I want to stuff a shoe in my mouth. The look on her face tells me that I've hit a nerve. It was not my intention to hurt Grace.

Grace wills herself not to cry. Veronica and Estelean feel the tension and politely leave. It's just Grace and me.

"I'm sorry, Grace. I wouldn't hurt your feelings deliberately."

"I think sometimes you hate me," Grace says. I deny it, of course.

Grace looks away. "I want to go to that concert more than anything, but I can't go in any of the dresses I own. And there's no extra money for me to buy a new dress. Jane never got to go, so why should I be treated differently?"

"I've got an idea!" I grab Grace's hand and bound up the back steps yelling, "Mama, Mama!"

It doesn't take any time for me to convince Mama to make a dress for Grace. She found a piece of pale blue taffeta left over from making Easter dresses for the pastor's girls.

"I think I have a pattern here for a cute dress that will look darling on you," Mama says, smiling.

Granny sent my dress at Easter. It's a rose-colored floral print with a square-cut neckline and sleeves that are cut in the shape of a leaf on a flower. I love it, although it's girly. But that's okay. I'm beginning to like a frill now and then. Anyway with minor alterations on my dress, I'm good to go.

Mama busily measures Grace. Looking at herself in the floor mirror, Grace can hardly talk without giggling. Meanwhile, I'm listening to the ball game between Milwaukee and St. Louis. "Wouldn't it be great if they showed ball games on TV? Now that would make owning a television set really worthwhile," I announce.

■   ■   ■

The concert is scheduled for May 1. Among the students who have been selected to play with the St. Louis Orchestra, Keith Winston, Kevin's oldest brother, a junior at Kirkland High School, is one of them. Keith is first-chair saxophonist in the band, but he also plays the organ and piano for our church youth choir. We've always known he's a musical genius, but it sure feels good when other people recognize it, too.

Mrs. Denapolis sent home the permission slips for the short bus ride to the park weeks ago. You'd think we were going to California instead of a mile down the road.

Then there is only one week left. Saturday before the concert, Mama sends me to Miz Lilly Belle's shop for a wash and press. "Can I get curls, Mama?" I ask.

"May I," she corrects my English, then answers, "No, you may not wear your hair down. You're not ready yet."

"I'm ready, Mama. You're not ready," I say, coming dangerously close to sassing.

Her eyes don't darken, so I haven't gone too far. "A mother's privilege," she says, smiling. And she actually looks happy. "You wait until you're a mother. Then you'll understand better.Until then, just trust me." Then off to the beauty shop I go.

Miz Lilly Belle's shop is packed. Seems every colored girl in the neighborhood is getting ready for the big concert. Everybody is talking about how wonderful it is that Keith's been selected to play with the orchestra. They're talking about their dresses and how they want to wear their hair. I'm pouting because Mama won't let me wear *my* hair down.

"I know yo' mama is gonna have you dressed like a wax doll," Miz Lilly Belle says, all the time telling me to hold my ear while she presses the edges. "You must be so excited."

"Not really," I answer in a huff. "I'd rather not go if I have to wear my hair in these sickening ponytails."

Suddenly, Miz Lilly Belle swings me around in the chair, so I'm facing her. "You listen to me, lil missy," she says sternly. "A whole lot of people fought hard for you to have the right to go to this concert. So you need to change your attitude and be happy you have opportunities we never had. Besides, you have plenty of time to wear your hair down. I'll fix you some nice bangs."

"Yes, ma'am." I reply, but I'm thinking, *Baloney!* Nothing can stop me from wanting to wear my hair the way Veronica Lake, the glamorous movie star, wears hers. One day I will.

I stop off at Mr. Bob's to buy a PayDay. He's excited about the concert, too. It never takes much for him to start talking, especially if it has anything to do with civil rights. The upcoming concert gives him the perfect opportunity to take off. I can hear the music in his voice as he tells me — for what seems the fiftieth time — about how long the Attucks PTA parents had fought with the school board about not including our students in the concert and the music competition. "It wasn't fair for our children to be excluded. The board always found some flimsy excuse or made hollow promises. Then they just stopped talking to us about it. Thanks to the Supreme Court, many former wrongs are being made right. And you and your friends are the beneficiaries of our work."

Mr. Bob is breathless when he finishes. "And just think," he adds with a big grin. "Keith is going to play with the orchestra."

At home, Mama is equally as thrilled. She's singing and sending up praises like she's in the middle of church service. Just as she finishes the hem on Grace's dress, the doorbell rings. It's Grace. "Right on time," I say, "your dress looks like something you might see in a fashion magazine."

Then I notice that Grace has been crying.

"Daddy won't let me accept the dress." Grace's bottom lip is quivering.

Mama doubles over in her chair and gasps as though she's been hit in the stomach with a fastball.

"Wait," says Mama, straightening up quickly. "I'm going to speak to Mr. Hamilton. Rosemary, you stay here."

"Mama, please don't make me miss out on seeing this," I say with pleading eyes. She gives her approval with a nod. With Grace and me in tow, she crosses the yard and knocks on the Hamiltons' door. I'm all the time wondering what Mr. Hamilton is going to do when he sees us.

"Well, yes," he says, swinging the door open. Grace scoots inside, but he stops us at the threshold. "What is this about?"

"I sew professionally for women of all races," Mama says. "I've put a lot of work into tailoring this dress for Grace. And I would like for her to have it." She holds out the dress. I am furious when he won't take it.

He shakes his head. "If my daughter needs som'thin' to wear, I'll buy it for her. We don't need charity."

Mama remains a lesson in how to be poised and dignified.

"I didn't think of it as an act of charity," she says. "But rather a neighborly deed offered with kindness and hopefully accepted in the same spirit."

Mr. Hamilton grunts.

Suddenly, Mrs. Hamilton appears at the door. "Tell you what," she says decisively. "How much would you charge for making a dress like that?"

"With the cost of the material and labor it would come to $3.50." Mama sounds very businesslike.

Mr. Hamilton looks disgusted. "I don't have . . ."

Mrs. Hamilton cuts him off. "I'll give you $3 for the dress. I'll pay you 25 cents now and 25 cents a week 'til I pay you off."

"Good enough for me," Mama says. The two women shake on it, and Mama gives Mrs. Hamilton the dress. We leave Mr. Hamilton standing there with his mouth open. Halfway down the walkway, we hear Grace squealing for joy. "Thank you, Mama. Thank you. Thank you. Thank you!"

"I thank you too, Mama!" I say.

May in Missouri is magical. Dogwoods, azaleas, daylilies, all blooming at once, make the garden at the park look like a wonderland.

All of us girls dressed in brightly colored dresses compete with the flowers for the attention of spectators as we make our entrance. I have on so many crinolines I feel like I'm floating.

Mrs. Denapolis is dressed in a lovely navy blue formal that makes her look like a queen. Mrs. Lancet looks like a principal in a long gray pleated skirt and a plain white top. But she is so proud of the way her students look that she's beaming.

The boys are standing around with buttoned-up collars and ties. I've never seen them look cleaner and more polished. They look miserable in blue, black, and brown pants, while we girls look like descending rainbows. Estelean is so pretty in her gold-colored dress trimmed in white lace. And I've never seen Gabe, Charley, or Kevin look so put together. One look at Mrs. Foxworthy with a shawl pulled around her shoulders, and I know what Estelean means when she says this has been a rough year.

I wave at my friends from Adams, but I have to stay with my Robertson class.

All the camera club members are taking pictures, including Mrs. Denapolis, but a real photographer from the *Post-Dispatch* singles Grace out and takes her picture. It will be in the paper the next day.

Years will pass and I will savor the sweet memory of strolling in that lovely garden with the sounds of Mozart playing in the background. And I will always remember the pride that I felt when Keith played with the St. Louis Symphony Orchestra.

But the best memory of all from my first Spring Concert is the delight of wearing my hair in looped Shirley Temple curls. At the last moment, Mama relented and let me wear my hair down.

I wake up the next morning to find something terribly wrong with Rags. She's wailing like a banshee. Mama and I stumble over each other, hurrying to see what's happening to her.

Mama knows immediately what's wrong. It takes me a minute to understand that Rags is getting ready to deliver kittens. We quickly get a box and fill it with towels. Rags hops in. And we wait . . . and wait.

By the end of the day, Rags is the proud mother of three adorable kittens — a female with black-and-white feet, a lion-colored male, and a black-and-brown leopard-looking male.

"You must be very proud of yourself," I tell her.

"Meow," Rags answers proudly.

After the concert, school is almost over. We're in the middle of tests, tests, and more tests. This time, I remind myself not to daydream and look out the window. But it is hard to concentrate with questions that seem pointless. Who cares what time it is if Sally is walking east and John is walking west? I'm ready when Saturday comes to forget books and just play. And I'm looking forward to summer break this year.

Daddy comes by the house often. To see me, he says. But I think he comes to see Mama, as well. "Must be something on TV you want to see, Mel," says Mama. Daddy laughs as he grabs a cola from the frig. They really are getting along better now that they are divorced. It's interesting how they manage to be friendly, although they aren't married.

I proudly show Daddy Rags and her new kittens. "That cat truly does have nine lives. She should have been dead," he says.

"She wanted to live," I say. "She hung in there and didn't give up! You shouldn't have either," I say. I wink and glance at Mama.

"You amaze me, baby girl," Daddy says. "I think you've been here before." Then he laughs and the sound is for real.

I can't believe it is Report Card Day again. Once more, things are not like they used to be. There is no gift for the teacher. No dress-up time. We're here in play pants and tops, even Mrs. Denapolis has on pedal pushers. But Mrs. Lancet has on a skirt. I can't imagine her in pants. That'd be like seeing a nun in regular clothes.

After Mrs. Lancet holds her last assembly, saying good-bye to us all, we go back to our classes to get our report cards.

"If you had to use one word to describe this year, what would it be?" Mrs. Denapolis asks the whole class.

Everyone begins chiming in.

Great.

Fun.

Interesting.

Hopeful.

"My word is *different*," I explain. "This has been a different place, different kids, and different kinds of friendships. In some ways I've been the one who is different. But now I know that different is okay."

"What's your word, Grace?"

"*Unforgettable.* I don't ever want to forget any of it or any of you, no matter where I live."

"Katherine? What about you?"

"My word is *change*. A lot of things have changed here and at home this year. And they are still changing . . . and will go on changing. It's scary sometimes . . . but I think I like it."

I can't say I've agreed much with Katherine, but I agree on this point. Things are changing. Maybe she will change her ways one day. Right now, she's still a hard pill to swallow. I'd like to meet her twenty years from now and see who she becomes.

"What's your word, Mrs. Denapolis?" Grace asks.

"*Special* is my word. This has been a special year with an extraordinary group of students. Of course, *tolerance* is the word I tried to teach all year, but that word can be defined by all the words we've used here today."

Stuart spoke up. "Next year, I'm going to a private school. But I'll never forget this year. I will try not to judge a person, a thing, or a place, without finding out the facts for myself."

Heads bob up and down in agreement.

"If I had to choose an animal to describe the feelings I have for this class and this year with you, I would choose the elephant," says Mrs. Denapolis. "The elephant is the largest animal I know. So I am elephant-happy," she says.

We all laugh.

Once again, it is time to give the report cards out.

When I say good-bye to Mrs. Denapolis, I am overcome with emotion, same as with Mrs. Washington last year, and I hug her around the waist. She hugs me back and adds a tight squeeze.

"I fully expect great things from you," she says, sounding like she's giving me an order. "Who knows, you might even be a doctor, lawyer . . . or educator . . ."

"What about president?"

Mrs. Denapolis smiles. But then she stops and looks me in the eye. "Rosemary Patterson, you are an American. So most definitely, you can be the president."

"But not before me," says Katherine the Great Mouth.

Summer is official now. Nothing to do until Labor Day.

All the other Attucks kids passed too. We'll all be at the junior high school together next year. All except Estelean. Her folks are sending her to Catholic school.

Grace and I are where we are most Saturday mornings at 10:00 A.M. We are listening to *No School Today* on the radio. Grace gives me a big hug for no reason.

"What did you mean when you said, 'no matter where I live'?" I ask her.

"I won't be here next year," she says.

I'm really surprised. "What? Where are you going?"

"Pop got laid off. So he's moving us back to Arkansas, where it is cheaper . . . and still segregated."

"It won't be segregated for long," I tell her.

"I think I'll like being back down South again," she says.

"The weather is better and the people are nicer in some ways."

The two of us sit on the porch, each one stroking a kitten, until I have to go inside for lunch.

"You can have one of the kittens," I say. "Then you'll always remember Rags."

"And you."

I know that I will never see Grace again when they move back South. She will probably not have a colored friend there, for sure. But I think she's learned something by being my friend. And I won't forget the different kind of friendship we shared.

Later, as I'm walking back from Mr. Bob's after showing off my grades — all A's — a familiar black Ford pulls up beside me. I know the car and wonder why Uncle John is parking in front of our house.

Then the back door swings open and I see a leg with braces on it getting out of the car . . . then a head. It's J.J. "You're home!" I'm shouting and running all at the same time. "J.J. is home!" I alarm the neighborhood.

People start pouring out of their houses to greet him — Mr. Bob, all the women in the beauty shop. Even Daddy comes from the shop when he hears J.J. is home.

It's so good to see all the Stenson family together after all these months. Mama and Aunt Betty can't stop holding onto each other and crying happy tears.

The therapy has worked. J.J. is able to walk with leg and arm braces. Even so, he's upright.

"I knew you could do it," I announce in my best sideshow

voice. "For I am the Wonderful Marveletta, assistant to the Great Marvellini. I know these things."

J.J. bows respectfully.

When all the excitement is over, we visit Rags and the kittens. "I gave Grace Hamilton one of the females," I tell J.J. "I hope that's okay with you."

J.J. shakes his head. "Can you imagine giving a Hamilton anything?" he says, picking up the black-and-brown leopard-looking male.

"Grace tries. She's still prejudiced, but she honestly tries. We did lots of stuff together like ice-skating and going to Mr. Bob's. We play ball with the boys and jump rope with the girls, and ride our bikes . . ."

He holds up his hand for me to stop. "So you two are best friends now?"

"Let me explain. Grace and I had a friendship for today. . . . But our friendship is for always. Even though you are a boy, you are my very best friend forever. Okay?"

"If you insist," he says, smiling.

"You gon' get hurt, boy, messing with me," I say. It feels so good to have my partner home again. Then I fill him in on all that's happened. "You would have enjoyed Mrs. Denapolis," I say, showing him pictures from the camera club.

Then it was his turn.

"I enjoyed my time with Mrs. Washington," he said. She got

herself certified as a tutor, so my grades could be official. I got A's and B's, too. My test scores are good enough for me to go to junior high next year."

"Won't that be fun?" I put in.

Rags comes and hops in his lap. He examines her wounds that have healed. "She's a wreck," he says, "but she's still going just like me."

"Rags wouldn't give up," I say, giving him a tap on his shoulder with my fist. "And neither can we."

"You know I'm going to have to wear these braces for the rest of my life," he says sadly. "That's what they told me at the hospital."

"The doctors are wrong. You will run and I will outrun you again," I put in.

J.J. chuckles. "Hey, that's right. The last thing I did before getting polio was beat you in a race," he says.

"You're never going to let me forget that are you?"

"Never!"

"Do you know how long never is?"

J.J. smiles. "As long as forever."

And that's a long, long time.

Author's Note

This is a work of fiction, but it is based in part on memories of my experiences as the only African-American child in my sixth-grade class, school year 1954–55, located in Kirkwood, a suburb of St. Louis, Missouri.

The story takes place at a time of great changes — when television viewing is coming and the sounds of radio are waning. It is a time when Dr. Jonas Salk's polio vaccine will eventually save many lives. But not in time to safeguard several of my childhood friends from suffering the horrors of the dreaded disease.

The Korean War has just ended, but the Cold War is beginning. The Soviet Union and the United States will remain locked in a thirty–year struggle, with the world poised on the brink of atomic destruction. I remember the frightening test drills at school in preparation for a nuclear attack. General Dwight Eisenhower, hero of World War II, has been elected president of the United States. And the Supreme Court has just passed down a landmark decision that overturns the "separate but equal" segregated system in American education.

Right away, the decision is controversial in white and black communities all over the country. In the Border States, such as Missouri and Kansas, the schools are integrated as soon as the decision is made. But in the South it will take decades for public schools to comply with the law.

Through a number of unexpected circumstances, I wind up being the only black child in my sixth-grade class. At the same time, my parents are separating and will eventually divorce.

This, then, is my story. I welcome you to share it with me. The attitudes, conflicts, and struggles that Rosemary experienced are a lot like mine. Rosemary represents in her form the lessons my parents taught me from an early age: to be proud but not arrogant, firm but not stubborn, humble but not subservient.

I have fictionalized the setting, characters, proper names, and events in order not to embarrass anyone and also to tell a good story. Rags, however, has not been altered. This book is as much a tribute to her survival as it is to my own during this difficult time in my life.

If this tough little black-and-white cat had not crossed my path at the time she did, my outlook on life might have been somewhat different. Rags was a healing entity for all who knew her. And when I am troubled, the memory of her still comforts me.

PATRICIA C. MCKISSACK
2006